Little House
on Rocky Ridge

When Pa and Ma and Mary and Laura were small, and before Grace was even born, Pa built a wooden house in Wisconsin. Later, when she grew up, Laura wrote about her childhood, beginning with the famous book *Little House in the Big Woods*. This was followed by six other books, ending with the one which tells the story of her marriage to Almanzo Wilder – *These Happy, Golden Years*. Later, she wrote the story of Almanzo's childhood in *Farmer Boy*.

Now, in *Little House on Rocky Ridge*, Laura's daughter Rose tells of how, when she was only seven, *her* mother and father leave their family in Dakota and make the long and difficult journey to Missouri, in a covered wagon, in order to start a new life.

Little House on Rocky Ridge

Roger Lea MacBride

Lions
An Imprint of HarperCollins*Publishers*

Little House is a registered trademark of
HarperCollins Publishers Inc.

First published in the US by HarperCollins Publishers Inc. 1993
First published in the UK in 1993
This edition first published in 1994

2 4 6 8 10 9 7 5 3 1

Lions is an imprint of HarperCollins Children's Books,
part of HarperCollins Publishers Ltd,
77/85 Fulham Palace Road, Hammersmith,
London W6 8JB

ISBN 0 00 674821 X

Printed and bound in Great Britain by
HarperCollins Manufacturing, Glasgow

For Joe Coday
A dear friend to three generations of the
"Little House" family and great citizen of
Mansfield, Gem City of the Ozarks

Contents

A Big Surprise

Rose jumped to her feet so fast, her stool toppled over. The book she was reading slid off her lap. Before she could grab it, it hit the floor with a loud thud.

Grandma Ingalls' head jerked up in surprise, and she laid down her sewing. "Gracious, child! You startled me."

"It's Mama!" Rose shouted. "I can hear her whistling!"

Grandma leaned forward to hear better. "So it is," she said. "Where did the time get to? Run and wake Aunt Mary from her nap while I put the kettle up for tea."

1

It had been hard for Rose to be good that day. Mama had promised a surprise when she and Papa came from work. Rose had tried to guess what it might be.

"Is it a dog?" she had asked Grandma. Ever since Nero, the big black Saint Bernard, had gotten sick and died, Rose had wanted another dog more than anything. But Grandma wouldn't tell.

Rose was so distracted by her curiosity that she had stitched her quilt pieces backward. She had spilled her milk, even though she was seven and a half years old. She had read the same page in *The Adventures of Robinson Crusoe* over and over and promptly forgotten every word!

She rapped on the closed bedroom door. "Aunt Mary, get up. Grandma is making tea," she called out. Rose ran back across the dining room to the open parlor window. The sweet spring air poured into the room, tangling the thin white curtains.

Rose could hear birds singing their hearts out. But clearer than them all was the sound of

Mama's whistling. Grandma often teased Mama for being unladylike. "Whistling girls and crowing hens always come to some bad ends, Laura," Grandma would say.

But Rose didn't care about Mama being unladylike. Mama whistled when she was happy, so hearing her always cheered Rose up. Not even a bird in spring could whistle like Mama. She whistled clear and sweet, trilling, chirping, or sometimes dropping the notes one by one, as a meadowlark drops them from the sky.

Rose spotted Mama walking with Papa. She held her skirt up from the dusty street and her bonnet swung on her back.

Rose greeted them at the door and got a big hug from Papa.

"Grandma's in the kitchen," Rose said. "And Grandpa went to see Mr. Boast." She looked for a dog but didn't see one. The surprise must be in Papa's pocket. But Rose couldn't see any bulges.

"Grandma made something special," said Rose. She took Mama's hand and pulled her into the kitchen. On the table was a platter of golden-brown pastries.

"Oh, Ma," said Mama. "You made vanity cakes."

Aunt Mary came downstairs and they all sat down at the kitchen table. Grandma poured tea for the grown-ups, and then she poured Rose a glass of cold milk.

Rose had never eaten a vanity cake. It was still warm when she bit into it. It was crunchy on the outside, but it wasn't sweet like cake. And inside it was air; just a bubble that disappeared the minute she put the cake in her mouth. Rose thought it was very clever, and delicious.

"These are perfect," Mama said. "Just the way you made them when we were little."

Rose tried to be patient, and not speak until spoken to, as they finished the rest of the cakes. Finally she couldn't wait another moment.

"Mama," she said, "what about the surprise?"

Mama's violet-blue eyes sparkled mischievously. "Well, it's a very big surprise," she said, glancing at Grandma. "Papa and I thought we should wait until after supper."

"Oh, no!" Rose begged. "Tell me now. Please?"

"I suppose now is as good a time as any," Papa said. "How would you like to go on a trip, Rose?"

"The surprise is a trip?" Rose looked at Mama in astonishment.

"Yes," said Mama. "A long trip. To Missouri."

"Missouri?" Rose had heard of Missouri one Sunday, when she played with Paul Cooley and his brother George. The railroad company was selling land in Missouri. It had given their papa a free ride to go see it. Mr. Cooley had brought back pictures of mountains and forests printed on shiny smooth paper. He had brought a huge apple from an orchard there. Mr. Cooley said those mountains and forests were called The Land of the Big Red Apple.

"Papa and I have decided to take you to Missouri," Mama said. "We will drive there, just as I traveled with Grandma and Grandpa when I was a little girl—in a wagon with the mares and colts."

Mama smiled and Papa twisted an end of his mustache. They looked at Rose, waiting for her to speak. But she didn't know what to say.

"Is it far?" she asked in a small voice.

"Yes, a long way from Dakota—er, South Dakota," Papa said. "I keep forgetting it is a state now. It will take us most of the summer to get there."

"Most of the summer?" Rose was shocked. What about Sunday dinners at Grandma and Grandpa's? How could she fetch ice cream from Barker's for Mrs. Sherwood and her sister? They always let her share. Then Rose shot a glance at Aunt Mary, Mama's blind sister, who now sat quietly, her hands folded in her lap. Aunt Mary had promised to teach Rose how to read Braille.

So many questions crowded into Rose's head, she wanted to ask them all at once. "Why are we going to Missouri? Are Grandma and Grandpa going with us? Are we going for long?"

Grandma's chair scraped on the floor as she got up to stir the coals in the cookstove.

"We're going to Missouri to live," Mama said gently. "We're going to make a new home there. But Grandma and Grandpa will stay here."

"But . . . why?" Rose asked. "Why do we have to go to Missouri? Why can't we stay here?"

"It's the drought, Rose," said Papa. "The prairie is turning to dust. People can't stay in a place praying for rain that never comes. Sometimes they must take matters into their own hands."

"In Missouri there is plenty of good water," Mama added. "And the winter is warmer, too. You know how Papa's legs ache so in the cold. Missouri is a new chance for us, Rose. To build a future. A future means a farm, with cows and sheep, and land for growing crops."

Rose didn't want Papa's legs to hurt. She wanted her family to have a future. Two winters had passed since they had moved into town. Before that, when they lived out on the homestead claim, there had been crop failures and bad weather and fire. For a time Mama and Papa had been dreadfully sick with a disease Rose could not pronounce: diff-theer-ee-ah. She had lived with Grandma and Grandpa, until Mama and Papa were well again.

Finally, when dry weather came to the prairie one summer and killed the wheat, Mama and Papa had to give up their homestead claim. The farm was a failure. Papa sold everything except the mares to pay their debts. They stayed in their rented house in town. Mama sewed for the dressmaker six days a week, for one dollar a day, and Papa hired out to do odd jobs. Sometimes he worked as a carpenter. For five weeks he served on a court jury and slept each night in the hotel.

"Remember on the homestead, when Trixy's colts ran free around the barn?" Papa said. "Remember Mama and me milking Harriet, and letting you have a drink from the pail?"

Rose nodded.

"Remember kittens and woolly lambs to

play with," asked Mama, "and the beautiful green grasses all around, waving silvery in the sunlight?"

Rose remembered. "Will we really have cows and sheep in Missouri?" she asked.

"Yes," said Papa. "Although perhaps not right away."

"But why can't Grandma and Grandpa come with us? And Aunt Mary. And Aunt Carrie and Aunt Grace?" Rose couldn't stop her voice from quivering.

Grandma turned from the stove. Her eyes were glistening. "There now, Rose," she said gently. "We have many friends here. Why, your grandpa is Justice of the Peace in De Smet. He was a founder of this town. We have our own house, and Aunt Mary to look after. Grandpa and I have made a future for ourselves right here."

Rose felt a lump rising in her throat. "Will we come back to visit?"

"Someday," said Mama. Now her eyes were glistening, too.

"We can always write to each other," Aunt Mary said cheerfully. "And we will think of you every day: Absent in body, but present in spirit."

Everyone was quiet for a moment. Rose sniffled without meaning to.

"Why, Rose Wilder!" Papa said heartily. "I'm surprised at you. We haven't even left yet! Going to Missouri will be an adventure. Just think of all the new places you'll see along the way! And in Missouri there are hills and orchards, and different wild animals. Wait until you see the trees! And Rose," Papa added, "the Cooleys are going with us."

"They are?" Rose shouted. "Paul and George, too?"

"Yes, of course." Mama laughed, and then everyone was smiling again. "Paul and George, too."

Rose felt a little better after that. She saw in the glow on Mama's and Papa's faces that going to Missouri would be an adventure. It made them happy just to speak of it. But when Rose thought of leaving behind Grandma and Grandpa, and her aunts, she still felt a hollowness inside.

Grandpa's Fiddle

The days were so full of talking and wondering about their trip that Rose forgot to feel sad. And she never tired of looking at Mr. Cooley's pictures of The Land of the Big Red Apple. There were rows of little trees in one. Another was of buildings that he said were a town in Missouri called Mansfield, Gem City of the Ozarks.

"Now I know three Miss states," Rose told Paul. "Miss-issippi, Miss-consin, and Miss-ouri."

"It isn't *Miss*-consin," Paul said. He was nearly ten years old and knew a great many things that Rose did not. "It's *Wis*-consin."

But Rose liked it better her way. To herself she still said Miss-consin.

Paul was the oldest. George was eight. As long as she could remember, they had been her friends.

Mr. Cooley owned two big covered wagons, and two teams of horses to pull them. Paul said he would drive one of them to Missouri.

"My pa says I'm old enough now," he bragged.

Rose could scarcely believe him at first. She couldn't imagine Paul driving a big team and wagon like the men in town. But she knew he wouldn't lie.

Papa and Mama's wagon was only a hack, with two bench seats. Now that they lived in town, they drove it mostly on Sundays.

"It's small," Papa said. "But it's sturdy and reliable."

"Can we really drive in it all that way, Manly?" Mama asked. Papa's name was Al-manzo, but Mama had nicknamed him Manly. "How will we ever fit everything in? How will we stay dry?"

"Don't you worry," said Papa. "I'll figure a way to beat the weather. And we don't own enough to fill a prairie schooner anyway. The fire in the claim shanty fixed that."

First Papa took out the wagon's backseat, to make room for the beds, trunks, camp stove, food sacks, folding chairs, and some wooden boxes. Then he nailed a post at each corner of the wagon-box. Over the posts he draped and tacked down a big piece of black oilcloth, to make a roof.

Then he made oilcloth curtains for the sides, the front, and back. The curtains rolled up on ropes. Papa could tie them to the roof when they weren't needed. At night and in bad weather, the curtains could be unrolled and tied to the wagon-box. When the curtains were down, the wagon became a snug little house on wheels.

Rose helped Papa paint the wagon-box and the wheels black, to match the curtains and the roof. Then the wagon gleamed like new in the bright sun. They all stood back to admire it.

"It'll be a tight fit," Papa said. "But there's

room for our big bed, with enough left over at one end to make a bed for Rose."

Rose wanted to sleep in it that night, but Mama said there would be nights enough to sleep in the wagon on the way to Missouri.

Summer dawned across the prairie. Fireflies rose from the grass at sunset, speckling the dusky air with their ghostly lights. The hard prairie winds blew hot and dry. In the fields around town the spring wheat that had shot up so green and hopeful a few weeks earlier stopped growing. Then it turned brown.

One morning Mama told Rose that it was their last day in De Smet. Rose helped her pack the trunks. At noon, after the dinner dishes had been washed and dried, they packed them away, too, in a wooden box. Mama tucked old newspapers between the plates to protect them. Then Rose helped Mama carefully wrap the cups. The beautiful willowware china would stay safely packed until they got to their new home. They would use tin plates and cups instead.

That night they all took baths, even though

it wasn't Saturday. Rose wriggled into her best calico dress. It was red, sprigged with tiny white flowers that looked like polka dots, and had a delicate lace collar Grandma had tatted for her last Christmas. Papa put on his Sunday suit and combed his hair and mustache. Then they all walked to Grandma and Grandpa's, being careful not to scuff their clean shoes or get them dusty.

Mama's face was radiant in the fading sunlight. She wore her black cashmere dress, with the white lace collar and the jet buttons down the front.

Papa stopped to pick two blossoms from a thicket of wild roses. He handed one of the pink flowers to Rose. "One for my little prairie Rose, who is leaving the prairie," he said. She held it to her nose and breathed in the sweet, fresh perfume.

Papa handed the other blossom to Mama. A smile scampered across her lips and she let out a tiny sigh.

"What is it, Bess?" Mama's given name was Laura. That was what everyone else called her. But Papa called her Bess, for Mama's middle name, which was Elizabeth.

"I was just thinking: I'm twice as old as I was when Ma and Pa brought my sisters and me to Dakota," she said. "There was only grassland then, as far as you could ride. And plenty of wild game. If only I had a poet's brain, or an artist's hand, to preserve those memories forever."

Rose tried to see the prairie in her mind, with no town, no dusty streets, no horses tied to the hitching posts switching their tails, no people walking, no dogs sleeping in the yards. But she couldn't imagine how it had looked when Mama and Papa first came there.

Grandma was cooking when they arrived. She looked as neat and tidy as she did in church. Her hair was parted in the middle, plaited, and wound into a tidy knot at the back of her head. Into the knot she had stuck her favorite shell comb.

Rose loved Grandma's comb. Every morning, as long as she could remember, Grandma had fixed her hair the same way, then tucked the shell comb into the knot. But now Rose realized that she wouldn't be there to see it anymore.

Suddenly she missed Grandma terribly, even though they hadn't left yet. She wrapped her arms around Grandma's waist and squeezed hard. Grandma's warm apron smelled of all the good things cooking in her kitchen, of pie and bread and chicken. Rose didn't ever want to let go.

"Goodness!" Grandma said. "A bear couldn't hug any tighter."

Grandpa came in from feeding his horses. Aunt Mary stirred the gravy in the pan. Aunt Grace and Aunt Carrie, Mama's younger sisters who still lived at home, set the table. The cozy sounds of clattering plates and ringing silverware mixed with their bright, laughing voices.

Finally Grandma served the platters and bowls of steaming food. There was fried chicken, a pitcher of smooth rich gravy, a bowl of mashed new potatoes with a golden-brown crust, and a bowl of bright-green spring peas. And a fresh baking of bread.

When Grandma was ready to pour the tea, she glanced at Rose and winked. "You know, Laura," Grandma said to Mama, "it wouldn't hurt for once for Rose to try a cup of tea."

"Yes, of course, Ma," said Mama. "After all, she's getting to be a big girl. And this is a special occasion."

Rose had wanted to drink tea for the longest time. When she was little, in the winter, Mama sometimes let her drink cambric tea, which was hot water and milk, with only a taste of tea in it. She had never drunk grown-up tea.

She could hardly be still while Grandma set the cup on its saucer. She impatiently kicked her legs as Grandma poured the golden-colored tea and added a cloud of milk.

Rose took the cup in her hands and carefully sipped the steaming liquid. It wasn't sweet, and it wasn't sour. She took another sip.

"Well, Rose," Mama said. "How do you like it?"

"It tastes like . . . tears, I think!" She put

the cup down with a little rattle and made a face. The grown-ups laughed.

"Maybe it needs a little sugar," Grandma said. She stirred in a spoonful of brown sugar. Rose sipped again, but then she didn't drink any more. She didn't see why grown-ups liked tea so well.

The talk around the table grew quieter. Mama touched Aunt Mary's hand as she spoke to her. Papa spoke to Grandpa in a quiet, respectful way, not hale and hearty as usual. And Grandma kept looking at Rose and asking her did she have enough to eat?

Rose thought about no more suppers at Grandma's. Her eyes stung. A hard lump rose in her throat. She was glad she didn't have to speak.

After the dishes were cleared, the family went out on the narrow front porch. Gentle breezes brought the sweet smell of warm grass. The only light came from the faint starshine.

Then Mama said to Grandpa, "Pa, would you play for us, one more time?"

"Why, yes, if you want me to," Grandpa said. "Run and get my fiddle, Laura."

Mama brought the fiddle box and laid it in Grandpa's lap. He took the fiddle out and twanged the strings with his thumb, tuning them up. He rubbed rosin on the bow.

Rose could see the glimmer of Grandpa's eyes and his long beard lying dark against the white of his shirt. His arm lifted the bow, and out of the shadows came the trembling voice of the fiddle, happy and strong and reaching. Then it was quiet again.

Grandpa tightened a string and twanged it. "Well," he finally said. "What shall I play? You first, Laura."

"Let Mary choose first," Mama said quietly.

"'Ye banks and braes of Bonny Doon,' please, Pa," said Mary.

So Grandpa played, and the grown-ups sang along. It was a song he had played and sung for Mama and her sisters when they were little girls, when they were the first settlers in the little town on the prairie.

"Ye banks and braes of Bonny Doon,
 How can ye bloom sae fresh and fair?
 How can ye chaunt, ye little birds,
 And I sae weary, full of care?"

Rose hummed. She didn't know the words. Then Grandpa played another song and then another. Rose knew some of them from Mama's whistling and singing. Sometimes the fiddle sang happily. Sometimes it sang so sadly, Rose thought her heart might burst open, like a bud.

After the fiddle had sung a long time, Grandpa stopped. "You folks'll be starting pretty early," he said to Papa. "And I see the moon has risen."

"If it's your pleasure to play, sir, we have till sunup," Papa said. "We only live once."

So Grandpa raised the fiddle and played on into the night. Rose was wide awake, listening, singing, and watching the grown-ups.

Finally the fiddle sang the last tune, "Tenting on the Old Campground."

> *"We're tenting tonight on the old campground,*
> *Give us a song to cheer*
> *Our weary hearts, a song of home,*
> *And friends we love so dear."*

Then Grandpa laid the fiddle in its box and put in the bow. Mama came to carry it back into the house, but Grandpa stopped her.

"Laura, you have always been dear to us, from the time you were a little half-pint half drunk up," he said. "Your ma and I never could do as much for you girls as we wanted. There'll be a little something left when we're gone, I hope. But I want to say now, I want you all to witness that when that time comes . . . well, Laura, I want you to have the fiddle."

From the darkness where Mama stood, Rose heard a coughing sound. Then Mama said, simply, "Oh, Pa."

Papa, Mama, and Rose were quiet as they walked back to their empty house, with the wagon loaded and waiting out front to take them away. The moon was high. The grass was silvery with dew. Their shoes made lonely clumping sounds on the wooden sidewalk.

Papa put his arm around Mama's shoulder and said, "Don't cry, Bess."

"I'm not crying," Mama said quickly. "I'm only . . . remembering. Pa played us to sleep with that fiddle when I was little. It's my first memory. He played by all those campfires and through blizzards and drought and sickness. We never could have gotten through it all without Pa's fiddle."

"Music does put heart in a body," said Papa.

The whole curve of the sky was filled with moonlight over the flat dark earth and the dark houses. The air had the sleepy feel of the still of night. But soon it would be morning.

When the sun had climbed high over the prairie, they would be gone, Rose thought, on their way to find a new home.

The Indian Story

In the gray light before sunrise, they drove the wagon to Grandma and Grandpa's house to say good-bye. Rose was so tired that it seemed like a dream. She hugged her three aunts and Grandpa twice, and Grandma three times. Then she climbed sleepily up over the wheel and onto the seat, between Mama and Papa.

The mares, Pet and May, were hitched to the wagon. Their colts, Little Pet and Prince, both four months old, stood beside their mothers sniffing the fresh morning. Papa tightened the reins and raised his hat. Everyone cried out all at once, "Good-bye!" "Good-bye!" "Don't forget to write." "I won't." "You be sure to." "Good-bye!" Then they were on their way.

Mama and Papa fell silent as the mares pulled the little black wagon down the street. Only the jingling of the harness, and roosters crowing in backyards, broke the quiet. At the end of the street, they turned onto the main road south. The colts pranced alongside, glad to be stretching their legs.

When they had passed the last house in the little town, they caught up with the Cooleys. Papa stopped behind Paul's wagon.

"Howdy, Mr. and Mrs. Wilder," Paul shouted to Mama and Papa. George sat next to him. Mr. Cooley drove the other big wagon, in front, with Mrs. Cooley beside him. Papa waved to Mr. Cooley, and the three wagons began their long journey.

But Rose's eyes wouldn't stay open any longer. Mama fixed a spot in the back, among their belongings, where she could lie down. Rose took one last look back at the town. Then she put her head down and fell into a deep sleep.

———

The sting of the hot sun on her face woke Rose up. Voices were singing.

"'Oh Su-sanna, Don't you cry for me!'" sang Papa.

And Mama answered, "'I'm go-ing to Missouri, With my washpan on my knee!'"

Rose sat up and rubbed her eyes. She looked all around. The wagon trail stretched behind them to the brown horizon. The wind blew a plume of dust away from the wagons. The little town was gone! Now there was only rolling prairie, a farmstead here and there, and a spinning windmill, all baking in the sun. Some men were harvesting a field of stunted wheat.

"Where are we?" she asked.

"We haven't gone far," Mama said. "Come sit with us and sing awhile."

Rose climbed over the back of the wagon seat.

"What shall we sing?" Mama asked. "How about 'The Rattling Wheel'?"

"Which one is that?"

"It goes like this." Mama began, and then Papa joined in.

"I remember," Rose said. Then they all sang it together:

> *"The stars are rolling in the sky,*
> *The earth rolls on below,*
> *And we can feel the rattling wheel*
> *Revolving as we go."*

Then they sang a modern song, "Ta-ra-ra-boom-de-ay," that Rose had learned in school. Rose liked it so well, she begged them to sing it again. When they had sung the last note, Rose started to sing it again from the beginning. Mama and Papa joined in.

At the end, there was a moment of silence. Mama and Papa looked at Rose as if to say, Enough is enough. But Rose couldn't resist. With a giggle she started over again. Mama and Papa laughed, and then they joined in, too.

"Ta-ra-ra-boom-de-ay, Ha-ha-ha-boom-de-ay." The music and the laughter carried Rose away, as light and free as a cloud.

The mares plodded toward the brown horizon, wavy and shimmering in the heat. Prince raced ahead, the wind rippling his glossy mane and tail. Then he stopped and stamped his foot, impatient for Little Pet and the mares to catch up.

All morning Papa's strong, veiny hands gripped the lines. The mares' heads nodded in time with their steps. The harness straps slipped back and forth along their shoulders. The checkreins lifted and fell above their manes.

Each dip of the road took them through a hollow where Rose could see nothing but dried grass and wildflowers nodding in sunshine. At the top of the next swell, the horizon was still brown and wavy, and far away.

When the horses crowded too close behind Paul's wagon, Papa never raised his voice. He never laid a whip to them. "Easy, now," he said. Pet and May listened, their ears twitching this way and that like birds on a fence. Horses trusted Papa.

Rose trusted him, too. Papa was always patient and gentle, even with strangers. He was always cheerful. She loved the tiny half smile his mouth made, partly hidden by his neatly clipped mustache, and the little laugh wrinkles that crowded around his blue eyes.

Rose knew that nothing could hurt them as long as Papa was there.

She wished Paul and George would turn around and wave to her. Through the arch of their wagon cover she could see the brims of their straw hats fluttering in the wind. The straps of their overalls crossed the backs of their sweaty gray shirts. Their bare legs dangled below the seat.

"That little shaver knows how to drive," Papa said. "That's a powerful team he's handling."

Rose remembered that Paul and George were not to play, ever, while Paul was driving the wagon. Mr. Cooley had told them that, in his deep, stern voice. Paul and George had answered him, "Yessir." "Yessir."

Finally Rose was tired of singing. She begged Mama to tell a story. "Tell about when the wolf almost ate you and Aunt Carrie," she begged.

"You know as well as I, that wolf never almost ate us. And I've told that story so many times," said Mama. "Maybe there's another I can think of."

"Here's one," Papa said. "How about the time old Dr. Thorne found that Indian mummy?"

"An Indian mummy?" Rose asked.

"Manly, I'm not sure—" Mama began.

"It's a harmless story, Bess," said Papa. "No one got hurt."

"Tell me! Tell me, please!" Rose shouted.

"I don't want you giving her nightmares is all," said Mama. "But I suppose."

So Papa began, "It was a little papoose, an Indian baby that had died. Dr. Thorne—he doctored the railroad hands—discovered it one day, way out on the prairie, way past the end of the tracks, where no white men had been. It was a scientific discovery. Those Indians had mummified it somehow, dried it out, and put it in that tree. That was their custom instead of burying their kin.

"Well, Doc Thorne was going to send it to

the Smithsonian Institution in Washington, or maybe sell it to Barnum's Museum. He showed it to me on his way to the depot."

"What did it look like?" Rose asked.

"I guess you'd say it looked like a little old man," Papa said. "It was wrapped in some cloth. Its skin looked like some kind of dark wood. It still had its black hair and eyelashes, too.

"Well, it wasn't too long before the Indians found out about it. And they were none too pleased. I was working in the railroad camp one day when four hundred of them showed up. They surrounded the whole camp at dawn and surprised us.

"The Indian chief told the camp boss to get that mummified baby back in three days, or there'd be trouble. Those Indians were on a hair trigger. The whole countryside was in an uproar. Homesteaders sent their families into town, and you couldn't find a spare bullet for anything.

"By that time, Doc Thorne had already caught the train to Tracy. I went into town to the depot and telegraphed down the line, trying to get ahead of him. We were lucky. He was just about to put that papoose on an eastbound express. But when he heard about the Indians, he got on the next train headed back west to us.

"When that train got in, I saddled up with the mummy and rode the twenty miles to the railroad camp. I could see from far away that the Indians were swarming through the camp like ants."

Rose gulped.

"All of a sudden, here comes one of their young warriors, up out of a hollow. He seemed to just appear out of thin air. He was all painted up and riding a pony with no saddle. Just riding it as fast and free as can be, straight at me. He and that pony moved like they were one animal. He was aiming his rifle right at me, too.

"I hardly had time to think. I didn't know what might happen next. But all he did was ride past, quick as a flash. I reckon he wanted to scare me, and he did a fine job of it, too.

Then he turned around and rode back to the other Indians in the camp, yelling something fierce."

"What did you do?" Rose asked.

"Why, I rode into the railroad camp as quick as I could. The boss came and took the mummy back to the Indian chief. Then the Indians rode away, as peaceful as sheep."

Rose wanted to see an Indian mummy.

"There aren't any more Indian mummies around here," Mama told her. "Or Indians, either. The soldiers made them move west, when the country was settling up."

Rose was sorry there weren't Indians to see. She would have liked to see a painted warrior riding his pony. But Mama said she had seen enough Indians in her lifetime, thank you.

"Tell me another story about Indians," Rose begged. "Please?"

"Not now," said Mama. "It's nearly noon—time to stop for dinner."

Dust Storm

The three wagons pulled up to a lone tree in a hollow. Everyone was thirsty, but there was no stream and no farm nearby to ask for water. So they drank from the water barrel tied to Paul's wagon. Paul stood in the wagon-box and lifted up the barrel's wooden lid. He reached for the dipper.

"Jiminy!" he cried out, dropping it. "That's hot!" The metal handle had been baking in the sun all morning. Paul wrapped his bandana around it so he could dip water for each of them. The water was warm and it tasted stale, but Rose was too thirsty to care. She drank so

34

greedily from her tin cup that she spilled some on her dress.

"Take your time, Rose," said Mama. "The horses have yet to drink, and we can't afford to waste a drop. We don't know when we might find more."

Paul filled two wooden buckets, for Rose and George to carry to the horses. Rose's bucket was heavy. It banged her shins, and the water sloshed out. She walked very slowly to keep from spilling more.

Papa and Mr. Cooley had unhitched the teams. They held the halter ropes while the horses lay down in the dust and rolled away the sweat and tiredness from their backs. Then Papa and Mr. Cooley tied the horses to the wagon wheels and put on their nose bags of oats. The colts nursed, and Papa also put some oats on the ground for them to munch. When it was gone, they nibbled the grass nearby.

Rose helped Mama and Mrs. Cooley unpack the dinner baskets in the shade of the tree. Grandma had made up a basket of fried chicken, hard-boiled eggs, bread with jam, and bread-and-butter pickles. Then they all sat down to eat. It reminded Rose of a Sunday drive to Lake Henry, without Sunday's clean clothes and proper behavior. She hoped she could play with Paul and George after dinner.

Mama sighed. "It's good to sit in the shade, on the soft grass. I can still feel the wagon seat bumping along."

The warm air quivered with the chatter of crickets and grasshoppers. Even in the shade Rose was hot, almost too hot to eat. She sucked on a pickle.

"How far have we gone now?" she asked.

"We're so close to home," Mama said, "you wouldn't guess we aren't going to turn around."

"The horses know we aren't," Papa said, taking off his hat to mop his brow. "They seem eager to put the miles behind them. I have to hold them back some, even in this heat."

"Maybe they can smell the water in Missouri," Mama said. "I'm eager to get there, too. All those bubbling springs you saw sounded lovely, Mr. Cooley."

"That's right, Mrs. Wilder," Mr. Cooley said. "You folks haven't seen a thing like it. You can't ride a half mile in the Ozarks without finding a spring or a creek of the purest water you ever swallowed. Just bubbling up out of the ground, free as you please."

"How I look forward to the forests!" Mrs. Cooley added. "I was raised back East, and I can say it, now that we're leaving: I never did like the emptiness of this land. There's just no comfort to be found in it."

Rose looked around them. The tree they were sitting under was an island of green in a sea of brown grass. Dust devils whirled along the road, spun twisting in the grass, and vanished with a flutter. Rose could not imagine water just pouring out of a hole in the ground. Or a land covered with trees.

That afternoon a dust storm came up on them from behind. A thick cloud of dust blew over them as they drove. The light dimmed, and the air was so thick that Papa could not see the wagon track.

"We'll have to wait it out!" he shouted over the roar of the wind. The Cooleys' wagons pulled off the trail, and Papa followed. Mama unrolled the oilcloth curtains and tied them in place. She and Rose huddled inside the wagon with kerchiefs over their mouths. Papa calmed and picketed the horses. Then he climbed into the wagon, bringing a gust of hot, choking air with him.

"It isn't so bad," he said, catching his breath. "The wind is hard, but there's light in the west. It ought to blow over soon."

The wind snapped and grabbed at the heavy oilcloth covers. The gusts slammed and jiggled the wagon-box. Mama picked up the thermometer in its wooden frame.

"Land sakes," she said in a voice muffled by her kerchief. "It's a hundred and two degrees."

The suffocating heat had softened the tarry black coating of the wagon covers. The odor of it stung Rose's nostrils. Her eyes itched. Her skin felt gritty, and her dress clung damply to her back. She could even taste the bitterness of the dust.

Finally, she could not be good a moment longer. "I'm thirsty," she said.

"Don't cry, Rose," Mama said gently, dabbing her neck with her kerchief. Her bangs lay limp on her forehead. "You must be a little patient, is all. What cannot be cured must be endured. Think how thirsty the poor horses must be, working so hard in this weather."

Rose did not feel better, or more patient. But she knew to keep her complaints to herself after that.

Finally the dust cloud thinned and disappeared. The sun shone brassy in a yellow sky. Dust had drifted in little piles on the wagon seat, and on every flat surface, and in every seam. Rose's blue-flowered calico dress and bonnet were grimy. When she stood up, dust shook from the folds in little puffs. Everyone's face was lined with dust and sweat. The horses were covered with it. The white feathers of the chickens in their wire coop, strapped to the tailboard, were frosted a pale brown.

Everyone was thirsty, but the water tasted muddy now. Only the horses drank it eagerly. Rose was sorry for them, having to stand outside in the blowing dust and then drink that muddy water. But she was sorrier for herself.

Making Camp

The wagons drove on into the hot afternoon, until the shadows of the horses and wagons began to lean far to the east. Then it was time to make camp for the night.

"There's a grove of trees up ahead, with a windmill nearby," said Papa. He shouted to Mr. Cooley and pointed. Mr. Cooley nodded and waved his hat. When they got closer, they could see a shanty, and water running from a spout into an overflowing trough.

"I'll go see about that water," Papa said, handing the reins to Mama. Mr. Cooley's tired horses led the three wagons into a tight huddle. Everyone climbed stiffly from the wagon seats to dust off, stretch, and look around. But only for a moment. There was work to do.

Papa came right back. "Fella says we can have all the water we want. Here, Rose," he said, handing her the wooden bucket. "Draw some fresh water for supper while Mama and I get out the stove."

Rose ran to the brimming trough and stuck her face right into the stream from the spout. Nothing had ever felt so refreshing as letting that water run down her chin and neck. She drank from the spout, paused for breath, and drank again. It was sweet water, and cold. Rose was sure she could never drink enough of it.

Then she remembered Mama and the horses. Rose quickly filled the bucket, but not too full, and carried it back to the wagons.

Papa and Mr. Cooley had unhitched the horses. Their work was done for the day, and they knew it. They rolled on their backs and squirmed happily this way and that. When they were finally cooled off, Papa and Mr. Cooley led them to the water.

"Now that we're traveling, your chores will be different," Mama told Rose. "First thing each evening is to find cook wood, if you can. Under those trees you ought to find some fallen sticks and branches."

Carrying water was hard work. But looking for wood sounded like a treasure hunt. Rose dashed under the trees. She was surprised to find George already there, dragging away a nice big branch toward Mrs. Cooley's stove.

It didn't seem fair to her that George had gotten a head start. But then she spotted part of a broken branch and picked it up. Some sticks were lying by a tree trunk. She picked those up, too. George saw Rose racing around, and he also tried to grab the biggest sticks first.

Hunting for wood became a game. Rose's legs rejoiced to be running after sitting cramped all day on the wagon seat. She tried hard to beat George to every stick. But they got to laughing and racing around so fast that they tried to grab the same stick. They crashed into each other, knocking themselves down and scattering their bundles.

"Hey, that's my stick. I saw it first!" George shouted.

"No it's not, either!" Rose shouted back. "I touched it first!"

"Rose!" Mama shouted.

"George Cooley, stop this instant!" Mrs. Cooley said sternly.

"That's enough, Rose," Mama called out. "I'm waiting for that wood to start supper."

Rose and George quietly picked up the scattered wood, although they could hardly know whose was whose. They carried the wood back to where the stoves were set up.

The little camp stove that Papa had made from sheets of iron squatted on the bare ground on stubby legs. Mama had fitted on the stovepipe. It stuck up in the air to keep the smoke from blowing in her face. The camp stove looked just like a cookstove in a house, only smaller.

Rose helped Mama break the sticks into

kindling to start the fire. Then she sat at the table in a chair and carefully peeled four potatoes. When she was done, Mama said she could watch Papa groom the mares.

Pet stood still while Papa combed and brushed away the sweaty harness marks. He brushed the dust from the fine, short hairs. He brushed over the sturdy shoulder muscles and the round flanks, down the slenderness of tapering legs. He brushed and rubbed until Pet's brown coat shone like satin.

"Can I help, Papa?" Rose asked. "Can I brush Pet, too?"

"She's a bit tall for you, Rose," Papa said. "And my brush is too big for your hand."

"Please, Papa!" Rose begged. "Just a little? I'll be careful."

Papa looked at Rose for a moment, his mouth half smiling, stroking his mustache. "Well, you're getting to be a big grown-up girl, aren't you? I suppose Pet might like to have her chest scratched a bit. Let me see. I think I have an old corncob in here."

Papa looked into the bag where he kept the

brushes. He fished out a cob.

"Pull it down, like this." He showed her. "You can use two hands, reach up high as you can, and pull down. Mind you always pull down. Don't push. And stay at her front," he warned. "She's a good gentle horse, but horses don't know their strength. She could kick you without meaning to."

Rose was excited—and nervous. She had never helped Papa with the mares before. But Pet stood still while Rose scratched her chest. Papa watched her as he combed the tangles out of May's forelocks.

"Don't be afraid to put some muscle in it, Rose. A horse has thick skin. And you can talk to her, too. Horses like to hear a voice. It soothes them."

Rose pressed down on the cob as she pulled it. The mare lowered her enormous head, murmured, and gently tickled Rose's ear with her lips. Little Pet stood close by, munching grass. Then the colt jealously poked her velvety nose in Rose's way.

"I can't think of anything to say," Rose said.

"Well, then, sing to her."

So Rose sang "Ta-ra-ra-boom-de-ay" to Pet. It was fun helping Papa. And she liked to see how Pet's hair lay in swirls and waves. But the best part was being near the colts. Rose thought horses, especially colts, were the most beautiful of all God's creatures.

"Little Pet wants to be combed, too, Papa."

"The colts aren't old enough," Papa said. "They are like children. Younger than you, Rose. They haven't learned the difference between right and wrong. But here's a bit of carrot you can give her."

Rose remembered to hold her hand open wide, so Little Pet wouldn't bite any fingers by mistake. The colt's breath whooshed warmly in her palm. Her bright eyes looked at Rose shyly. Then she reached out and took the carrot. Rose heard three crunches, and it was gone. Little Pet nuzzled her, looking for more.

Rose loved the frisky way the colts played and chased each other. She loved their long slender legs, and the nervous way they tossed their heads. And there was a trembling, terrifying wildness about them that Rose also loved. Their hearts were strong and as free as the prairie itself. Just watching them gallop across the broad flat land, their manes and tails fluttering, made Rose's heart soar .

Finally, Mama and Mrs. Cooley called suppertime, and the families came together to eat. Mama had fried salt pork to go with beans and fried potatoes. The grown-ups ate at Mama and Papa's table. Rose sat on one of the wagon tongues with Paul and George, balancing her tin plate on her knees. Everything tasted delicious. Mama said hunger was the best spice.

"Yes, ma'am," Mr. Cooley said cheerfully. "Even dirt tastes good when you're camping."

"You best not be speaking of my cooking," Mrs. Cooley fussed. "Or maybe dirt is just what you'll get!"

"Now, Emma, I only meant . . ." Mr. Cooley stammered. "Well of course your cooking is fine. Just fine. These dumplings are delicious. And you know how I go on so about your apple pie."

Papa's mustache quivered, and his eyes

twinkled. Mama cleared her throat and stood up quickly. "Rose, help me with these dishes, please."

After the dishes were washed, Mama said Rose could play. "Until dark. Then straight to bed."

The children explored in the little grove of trees, with Mr. Cooley's black-and-white herd dog, Ben.

"Did you see that big blacksnake by the road today?" Paul asked. "Gosh, it must have been ten feet long. I thought for sure the horses were going to bolt. But they didn't even flinch."

Rose told Paul and George Papa's Indian mummy story.

When they were tired of talking, they played fetch with Ben. Then Paul said they should have a race.

"First one to that fence post over there!" he shouted. They raced each other through the grass. Paul was taller and his legs longer. He won easily. But Rose knew she could beat George if she really tried. She touched the fence post just before he did.

"I beat you! I beat you!" she panted.

"Did not either!" George shouted, his face red. "My foot was in front of yours. Touching doesn't count. I beat you!"

But Rose knew she had been faster. It was naughty, but part of her enjoyed teasing George.

They played together until all they could see of each other were the pale spots of their faces, hands, and feet. The only light in the sky was a thin band of deep purple at the horizon. Then Mama called Rose for bedtime.

Rose climbed into the wagon to put on her nightgown. She saw that Mama had made her bed up in front of the wagon seat. The wagon boards on three sides made it as cozy as a crib.

Behind her little bed, Mama had made the big bed on top of the bedsprings, which were on top of the trunks packed with all the things they wouldn't need until they got to Missouri. Rose's trundle bed was also under Mama and Papa's bedsprings.

Rose wriggled into her covers. Papa blew

out the lantern. Then, from the darkness, came all the little night sounds, curling around Rose like a blanket. The chickens fluttered sleepily in their coop beside the wagon; the cooling night air whispered in the grass; and over it all the crickets chirped a steady chorus.

Then Rose heard a new sound, high-pitched yapping and howling, far off in the distance. She had never heard anything so lonely and haunting. Her scalp crinkled. Ben barked twice from his bed under Paul's wagon.

"What was that?" Rose asked the darkness. "Is that wolves?"

"It's just coyotes," said Mama. "There are no wolves here. Go to sleep now."

Rose was tired, but she could not make her thoughts go to sleep. It had been such an exciting day. She couldn't wait to tell Grandma, and Aunt Mary, and . . .

But then Rose remembered: There was no one to tell things to. They weren't going back. Their whole lives were in that wagon now.

The coyotes began yapping and howling

again. The wind slapped and tugged at the curtains. Rose huddled down in her little bed and turned her face to the wagon boards. She could feel her heart beating in her ears.

The Writing Case

A rooster crowed nearby. Rose opened an eye. Fingers of faint gray light reached in through the curtain corners. A bucket clunked, and then she heard water being poured.

"Good morning, ladies," sang Mama's voice. The chickens clucked an answer.

Rose's other eye popped open, and she sat bolt upright. The new day had started without her! She bounded out from under her covers and wriggled into her dress as quickly as she could. Then she sat on the wagon's endgate so Mama could button up her back.

"Wash your face and hands in the wash-basin," Mama said. "Then come sit on the wagon tongue so I can brush out your hair."

Papa was beating pancake batter. Salt pork sizzled cheerfully in the pan. Mama plaited Rose's long brown hair into two braids. Rose swished her bare feet back and forth in the cool, dewy grass. She watched the sky's dark edge slowly turn pink. Paul and George walked by, carrying buckets of water to the horses.

"Mornin', Rose," Paul said.

George huffed and puffed, his bucket sloshing over its sides. Rose wished Mama would hurry, so she could water the horses, too.

"Be still," Mama said. "I'm nearly done."

Papa took out the salt pork and tested the iron skillet with drops of water. The drops danced, so he knew it was exactly hot enough to cook the pancakes without burning them.

Papa poured batter for one large pancake, as big as the skillet. Dozens of little bubbles rose through the batter. When the bubbles were bursting with little puffs of steam, he flipped the pancake over. The bottom was perfectly golden. In a minute, Papa peeked under its edge. Then he flipped the smoking pancake onto a plate with one smooth motion. That was the blanket cake.

Next he poured out the batter into three smaller cakes. In no time they were done, too. He drizzled the smaller cakes with some melted brown sugar and tucked them under the blanket cake, to keep them warm. Then he poured batter for three more pancakes.

Finally, Mama finished plaiting Rose's braids, and they ate. The bites vanished, sweet and light, as soon as Rose put the fork into her mouth.

"It carries me back through the years, traveling this way," Papa said. "It puts spring in a man's step and hope in his heart."

"Lately the past has been stepping all over the heels of the present," said Mama. "This morning I could almost hear my ma's voice, calling me to wash for breakfast."

Rose helped scrape and clean the dishes. Then she helped Mama repack all the things they had used for camping. They stowed the table and the chairs, the camp stove, the hammock that Aunt Mary had netted for them, tin plates and cups, frying pan, coffeepot, washbasin, water pail, picket ropes and pegs, and the salt pork and sack of flour, as well as the sacks of corn and the oats for the horses.

Mama laid the last sack inside the endgate. "Now for my writing case, Rose. It's on the wagon seat."

Rose loved Mama's writing case. Papa had made it for her one winter. The polished wood was as smooth and rich as well-oiled leather. Rose never could resist stroking it, although she was not supposed to touch it unless Mama said so. The case opened like a book, with the two sides hinged together. When the case lay all the way open, it turned into a little slanted desk for Mama to write her letters on. Two compartments were hidden underneath the slanted surface. That was where Mama kept her paper and envelopes.

Rose carefully handed the case to Mama.

She started to put it away. But then she stopped.

"Come sit here, on the endgate," she said in a solemn voice that surprised Rose. "Do you think you can keep a secret?"

A tingle of excitement ran through Rose. It was the first time Mama had ever shared a secret with her. "I can keep it," she said. "Is it a secret from Papa?"

"Papa knows," Mama said. "The secret is what's in my writing case. It's the money I saved all last year, from sewing for the dressmaker. I want you to remember that. It is one hundred dollars, and it is here in my writing case. That one hundred dollars is our future, when we get to Missouri. Do you understand?"

"All those dollars are in there?" Rose asked. "How can they fit?"

"No, Rose. All those dollars are one piece of paper, called a hundred-dollar bill. It is hidden, under the envelopes and paper. You must never, ever tell anybody that it's there. And you must never play with the writing case. Do you understand?"

"Yes, Mama," Rose said solemnly.

"And you must remember one thing more," Mama said in her most serious voice. "If anything should ever happen to Papa and me, you must keep the writing case. Do you understand?"

"Yes, Mama." Rose was not sure she understood the part about anything happening to Mama and Papa. But she was afraid to ask.

"That's my good girl," Mama said, and stood up. "Now let me put the case away, and then let's get the chicken coop lashed to the endgate. I see Papa has the team hitched."

Finally the three wagons drove off into the new morning. The horses were rested and eager. The first rays of sunlight spilled buttery all across the prairie; chirping meadowlarks fluttered up from the grass. The ridges blazed gold, and all the low places were cast in long dark shadows. Smoke trailed from the chimneys of claim shanties and sod huts. Spinning windmills sprouted from the swells, peeked out from the hollows, or hid in clumps of trees.

The horses plodded, their black manes and

tails blowing feathery in the wind. The level country kept coming.

And Mama and Papa and Rose sang:

> *"O Dakota land, sweet Dakota land!*
> *As on thy burning soil I stand*
> *And look away across the plains*
> *I wonder why it never rains,*
> *Till Gabriel blows his trumpet sound*
> *And says the rain has gone around.*
> *We don't live here, we only stay*
> *'Cause we're too poor to get away!"*

Rose glanced behind her, into the wagon. They were not too poor to get away, she knew, as long as they had the writing case.

Covered Wagon Folks

It was near sunset when the wagons stopped for the night by a spring. The parched smell of heat and dust rose from the roadside. Papa climbed down to unhitch the mares. He put a hand on May to stroke her before unhooking the traces. Then he stopped, staring back, past the wagon cover.

"By golly," he said. "It looks like the whole of Dakota is moving."

Rose scrambled through the wagon to look out the back. "Mama, look!"

Along the road behind them, straight over the low curves of the prairie, covered wagons were coming. There were small groups of wagons, with spaces between the groups. They were coming as far as the eye could see. The wind blew away from those wagons a haze of dust that became a thin gold mist in the slanting sunshine.

"I guess hard times are driving them out too," Mama said. Her forehead wrinkled into little knobs of worry. "I wish we had taken another road, Manly. I don't like the idea of camping among covered wagon folks."

"Why, Bess. I'm surprised at you," Papa said. "Those folks might be company for us. Likely pretty good company, some of them. And after all, we're traveling in a wagon, too."

"You know very well what I mean," said Mama. "We know where we're going, and we're traveling with friends. But with all the country pulled up and drifting, and so much lawlessness and horse stealing, who can say what sort of people are about? Besides, there's Rose to consider. Goodness knows what she might see and hear."

"Well, we can't take another mile out of the

horses tonight," said Papa. "Tomorrow we'll see if there's another road."

Now all those covered wagons came crawling on up. They pulled creaking and jingling all around on the wild grass and began making camp. The empty prairie was suddenly as lively as a small town.

Campfires flickered to life as darkness crept over the grass. Rose heard pot lids clanging and many voices. She could smell all those good suppers being cooked. Horses whinnied and dogs barked. Ben barked back, until Mrs. Cooley scolded him. A man was shouting someone's name. Laughter broke out nearby. Somewhere a baby was crying.

Surrounded by the sounds and smells of all that living, Rose felt wonderfully alive.

"After chores, let's look around," Paul said at supper. "I bet there are fifteen wagons here. We could go around and count them."

Rose stole a glance at the table where Mama and Papa were eating and talking with Mr. and Mrs. Cooley. Rose wanted to go exploring with Paul and George.

But she didn't want to ask Mama if she could. She knew the answer. She wanted so much to know what Mama was afraid for her to see and hear. She balanced her tin plate on her knees and looked out at the golden points of light of the other campfires. She wondered what all those people were doing. She wondered where they were going.

After supper chores, Mama said Rose must stay close by the wagons.

"Yes, Mama," she muttered.

"That goes for you boys, too," Mr. Cooley said.

Rose kicked at a clump of grass with a bare foot. She didn't like to be told where she could play. But she went to sit with Paul and George by one of the wagons.

"Hey, Rose. Look what I can do," George said. He held his hand in a fist and looked toward the side of the wagon. Then he wiggled his hand.

"Not like that," Paul scoffed. "That's nothing at all." He held his fist in the air and wiggled it. "Look, Rose."

Rose looked at the side of the wagon, and there, in the lamplight, was the shadow outline of a rabbit's head, with ears and an eye and a nose. She giggled. Rose had never seen such a thing. Then Paul made a dog with short ears and a long nose. The dog opened its mouth and Paul barked. Rose laughed.

Paul tried to show Rose how to do it, but she couldn't get her fingers to look like ears and she couldn't figure out how to make her hands work together.

"Listen!" Rose said suddenly. Someone was playing a fiddle. She stood up and peered around the side of the wagon. Across the dark emptiness she could see the campfire where the fiddle music was coming from. She could make out people moving about the campfire. Paul and George were standing next to her, looking and listening.

"Come on," Paul whispered. "Let's have a look."

"But . . ." Rose started to say.

"Just a look," said Paul. "We'll come back so fast, no one will even know we were gone."

"But Paul," George whispered. "If Papa catches us, we'll get a licking."

Paul's mouth puckered in thought. Ben whined from under the wagon. He wanted to play, too, but Mr. Cooley had tied him to one of the wheels.

Finally, Paul said, "Aw, come on. We'll just walk a little ways. There's no harm in that."

"Well, you can go and get yourself a whipping," George said. "I'll just stay here."

"Stay then," Paul said. "Come on, Rose." Before she could think about it, Rose was following Paul out into the dark grass. George came after all.

They crept like Indians through the grass. Rose's heart pounded, and she looked back. But no one had noticed them leaving.

"Wait, Paul!" George whispered loudly. "This is too far."

"Just a little bit more," Paul said.

Rose could see the campfires all around her. But everything else was warm velvety darkness.

Suddenly a horse snorted right next to Rose,

startling her. She stumbled and fell. She got up quickly and looked back again. Her own campfire was far away now, an island in a black sea. Her thoughts fought each other; maybe she should turn back.

She could just make out the shapes of Paul and George ahead of her. They were still walking through the grass. She looked again toward their camp. But then Rose heard the music, and she dashed after Paul and George.

They were crouching in the tall grass, close to a covered wagon, just outside the light of the campfire. Rose could see a man sitting on a chair, playing the fiddle. He was tapping his foot. Some other men were sitting on the wagon tongue, clapping and singing to the music.

Near the campfire, a man and a woman were dancing. They danced in a circle, each with an arm hooked through the other's elbow. Every once in a while they stopped, hooked their other arms, and danced the other way. Each time they changed direction, the woman's long braid swung merrily and she laughed.

The sounds of the music and the singing and the clapping delighted Rose.

"Oh, the hinges are of leather," they sang,

"The windows have no glass
And the roof it lets the howling blizzard in,
And I hear the hungry coyotes
As they sneak up through the grass,
Round my little old sod shanty on the
*   claim!"*

"Are those covered wagon folks?" Rose whispered.

"Of course they are," Paul said. "Look. They have a wagon. And it has a cover. Just like ours."

"I know," Rose said. "But Mama said she doesn't like to camp among covered wagon folks."

"What's the harm in it?" Paul asked. "This is exciting. I never had so much fun as I'm having right this minute."

Rose looked at George, but he just shrugged his shoulders. She knew the hundred dollar bill had something to do with not being covered wagon folks. But she was not supposed to tell anyone about that. Still, she was confused. Those people singing and dancing did not seem dangerous. They did not look lawless, either.

The music changed. The fiddler played a new tune. The men sang:

> *"So if ever you're caught in any such scrap,*
> *Through being too timid or bold,*
> *Recollect, my friends, whose fault it is,*
> *And blame yourself if you're sold."*

Rose thought it sounded a bit naughty, but she wasn't sure.

The music stopped. The man playing the fiddle wiped his face with a kerchief. Then he looked up, right at them!

"Say! Who's that yonder?" he shouted, waving the bow. The other people around the campfire turned to look. A dog began to bark and ran toward them.

For a moment none of the children moved.

Then Rose grabbed Paul's shirt and pulled him. "We have to go back!"

"Come on over, neighbor!" the man shouted. He had a long gray beard and a red face. "Y'all come on over and sing with us a spell." The man stood up and took a step. "Why, it's jist a bunch o' young'uns," he said, laughing loudly.

Rose turned and ran as fast as she could toward the tiny light of their own campfire. She could feel the ground under her feet, but it was too dark to see where she was going. She just ran blindly. The grass whipped her legs. Her dress swished against it.

She didn't even notice Paul passing her. When she got back to the rear of their wagons, there he was, peering around the corner to see if any grown-ups had noticed.

Ben barked and wagged his tail joyfully.

"Shhh!" Paul said, a finger to his lips. Rose let herself drop into the grass. She could not go another step. Her heart beat all over her body. She gasped for breath. Then George came running up.

"That was fun!" he said. They all laughed.

"What was fun?" a deep voice boomed.

It was Mr. Cooley! Rose held her breath. He had appeared out of the air, large and square and powerful. He towered over them with his legs apart, hands on his hips.

Mr. Cooley waited for an answer.

"Nothing, Papa," Paul said, catching his breath. His eyes were big and round. "We were . . . only playing tag."

"That will be all for tonight," Mr. Cooley said. "You boys go on in the wagon and get settled."

Rose tiptoed past Mr. Cooley, then dashed to her wagon.

Mr. Cooley stared out into the night. There were only campfires to be seen, flickering in the distance.

At the River Crossing

The next morning Papa had a surprise for Rose. "Would you like to ride with Paul and George?"

"Could I?" Rose shouted.

"Yes," said Papa. "But you must behave. You mustn't distract Paul from his driving, or Mr. Cooley won't allow a next time."

"Yes, Papa," Rose said, trying to sound well behaved. Inside she was jumping up and down with excitement.

"Morning, Rose," Mr. Cooley said. He was holding the bits of the horses and smiling at her. "All ready?"

Rose nodded so eagerly that her sunbonnet fell back off her head. A big grin spread across Paul's face.

"Paul!" Mr. Cooley said sharply. "Keep those reins taut."

Paul's face fought a smile, but the corners of his mouth still quivered. He held the reins of the big black horses in his hands. Rose noticed that he hunched over and rested his foot on the dashboard, just the way Papa did. He pushed his hat off his forehead, to see better. Papa did that, too. It shocked Rose to realize how grown-up Paul looked.

Mr. Cooley lifted Rose up onto the high seat, and she settled herself down between Paul and George. Paul gave the reins a little flip and chirruped to the horses. Their heads began to bob as they pulled the wagon in line behind Mr. and Mrs. Cooley's wagon.

"Is it hard to drive?" Rose asked. A covered wagon was so much bigger than Papa's wagon. She was surprised to see how high off the ground she was.

"Not for me," Paul said. "My pa says I have a knack for it. One thing, though: You have to watch in case the team might shy from something. Like a snake. Horses hate snakes. You have to hold the reins just a certain way; not too tight, not too loose. Want to try?"

"Could I?" Rose asked in astonishment.

"Sure you can drive," Paul said. "You hold the ends of the reins like this, see. I'll hold on to the rest of them, just in case."

Rose took the warm leather reins in her small hands. But the lines still ran through Paul's hands. She wasn't really driving. But it was fun to pretend. She watched what Paul was doing. But she didn't see him doing anything, really. He was just sitting there, holding the drooping reins.

The three of them talked as they drove. They talked about everything under the hot, blazing sun. They counted jackrabbits bounding away in the grass. They laughed to see roadrunners dashing ahead of the wagon. They watched the hurrying clouds and took turns saying what they looked like. They wondered about the hills in Missouri, and whether they would go to the same school.

When they were tired of talking, George

and Rose played hull gull while Paul drove. They took five kernels of corn apiece from a feed sack in the wagon. Then they each took turns guessing how many kernels were in the other's fist. If you guessed wrong, you had to give up the same number of kernels as you were wrong. When you were exactly right, the other person had to give you all the kernels in his or her fist.

Rose guessed three. But when George opened his hand there were only two. So Rose had to give George one of her kernels, because she was wrong by one. Rose put her hands behind her back. Then she showed George her fist.

"Two," George guessed right, and Rose had to give George both kernels in her fist. Before long, George had all the kernels. Then they divided them up and started over.

Once, as they climbed a hill and the wagons were close together, Prince trotted right up to Paul's wagon and looked at them. Then he galloped away to his mother again.

"Gosh, he's beautiful," Paul said, looking

back around the cover of the wagon. "My pa says he's never seen finer colts. That Prince has a real fast look about him, too. I bet he'll be fun to ride someday."

The families stopped at noon in a grassy place by the wagon tracks, so they could eat their dinner. Rose gathered dead grass and weed stalks for a fire. Mama boiled water for tea. Then she got the hardtacks out of the wagon.

Hardtack was a biscuity kind of bread that Rose had not eaten before. Each piece was white and round, big as a dinner plate, and dimpled with tiny holes Mama had poked with a nail. She had baked them without yeast. They came out of the oven flat and hard as wood. Mama said hardtacks stayed fresh a long time, like crackers. She had baked a whole sack of flour into hardtacks before they left. As long as they had hardtacks, they would never go hungry.

"Now we're Israelites," Rose said.

"We are?" Mama said in surprise.

"In the Book of Exodus," Rose said. "The

Israelites had to eat bread that was . . ."

"Unleavened?" Mama helped, then laughed. "We are emigrating to a promised land. But that doesn't make us Israelites, Rose. We're still Congregationalists."

You couldn't bite into a hardtack, or break it easily with your hands. Papa had to smash it into smaller pieces with a hammer. Mama poured hot water into Rose's cup and showed her how to dip the pieces until they were soft enough to eat. The hardtack was soggy that way, but Rose was hungry and it tasted delicious.

After dinner, Mr. Cooley told Paul to switch places with Mrs. Cooley. "We're coming to a river crossing. I want those reins in experienced hands."

Paul's shoulders sagged. He shoved his hands into his pockets and kicked up dust as he walked to his father's wagon. Rose prickled with anger for him. Paul was a good driver. Papa had said so. It wasn't fair.

"May I ride with Paul and George tomorrow?" Rose asked. "I was good."

"You were good," said Mama. "You may ride with Paul and George again, but only when Mr. Cooley says so. You must not overstay your welcome."

"Wind's picking up," Papa said, craning his neck to look at the sky. Dark-gray clouds were piling up at the horizon. "We may get a bit of rain. At least it would lay this dust by."

They began to see other wagons, coming from several directions. They were all heading toward the river crossing.

"You see, Bess, all the roads are the same," said Papa.

"Yes," Mama said. "It seems the whole country is turned loose. It's a sin and a shame what the government in Washington did to folks, promising them free land. Free land, indeed.

"It only shows that no good ever comes of getting something for nothing. It nearly ruined my pa, and look what it did to us. Every soul ought to pay his way in this world. It's the only honest and true way to live."

Now their three wagons joined a longer line

of wagons. Here and there they passed the beaten-down spots of old campgrounds and the black circles of dead campfires.

Finally they crested a ridge. Spread before them was a great, winding river. Rose had never seen so much water. The river curved away in both directions as far as the eye could see. And it was wide.

"How will we get to the other side?" asked Rose.

"Do you see the ferry?" Mama said, pointing. "Do you see it, there in the middle?"

Rose could not see anything at first. Then she spied it. Looking no bigger than a chip of wood, or a leaf, the tiny ferry bobbed in the middle of the river. It slipped sideways as it fought the pull of the current, clinging to a rope that had been strung from one bank of the river to the other. She gulped. Something fluttered in her stomach. Rose realized she didn't know how to swim.

On the road before them, a long line of wagons waited for the ferry. When the first wagon in line boarded, the whole line crept one wagon closer. The line crawled across the flat land like a great long worm.

All afternoon they inched toward the river. There was nothing else to do but wait. The sun began to sink, but the wind blew hot as an oven. Dust flew as rolling, black clouds darkened the sky behind them.

Mama kept turning to look back at the stormy sky, her forehead furrowed with worry. The horses tossed their heads restlessly. They were hungry, and tired of standing in harness.

Rose grew itchy, too. "Mama, can I get down? I'm tired of sitting."

"'May I,'" Mama said. "Not 'can I.' No, you may not."

"It's getting late," Papa said. "Maybe we should pull off and camp for the night."

"I had hoped we would cross today," said Mama. "I don't like to camp in such a crowded place. And with this weather blowing up, who knows how long we might have to stay here."

"Look, Papa," Rose said. "The Cooleys' hens are thirsty." Their heads were sticking out of their coop, and they were panting.

"That's a sharp eye, Rose," Papa said. "I'll bet ours need water, too. We have to be mindful of that, or else we won't get them through." Papa gave the reins to Mama and got down from the wagon. He took the jug and filled the water dish in the Cooleys' coop, and then gave some to Mama's hens.

The closer they got to the front of the line, the more fluttery Rose felt. Dust and dry weeds hurtled past them in the wind. The closer to shore they got, the wider and nastier that river looked. It just stretched away, almost to the horizon.

"What river is this, Mama? Is it the Mississippi?" she asked.

"This is the Missouri, Rose."

"Is that Missouri on the other side, then? Are we there already?"

"No," Mama said with a tight chuckle. "The Missouri River is very long. The other side is Nebraska. When I was a little girl about your age, I crossed this river on my way with Grandma and Grandpa to Indian Territory. And it's no prettier now than it was then," she added.

The Big Muddy

The brownish-yellow water rolled along, lazy yet so powerful that nothing could stop it. It seemed to kill everything it touched. Trunks of dead trees stuck up from it. The dry land along the banks had rotted away from under the dead brushwood.

Rose could not see into the water at all, it was so murky. Mama said the Missouri had a nickname: Big Muddy. It was a name the Indians had given it. Just looking at that river would scare anybody.

Finally it was the Cooleys' turn to go on the

ferry. There was room for only one wagon at a time. It would take two trips to get both of Mr. Cooley's wagons across.

The sun was near to setting. Black storm clouds piled up in the sky. Brown, foamy waves curled up out of the river. The little ferry carrying the Cooleys' lead wagon and horses pitched and tossed on the swells. Mama, Papa, and Rose watched in fretful silence as it made the crossing and then returned to pick up the second wagon.

"So! That's Nebraska!" Papa finally said, loud and hearty. He was trying to fill the hollowness inside them all.

Suddenly a violent gust of wind slammed their wagon. There was a sickening shudder. Then Rose felt the wind lifting them off the ground, the whole wagon they were sitting on, into the air! An instant later it dropped the wagon down again. There was a terrible *BANG!* as it hit the earth. Rose's teeth clacked together. The pots and pans clattered crazily.

The colts began to squeal in terror. Pet and May whinnied and reared. They looked back

with wild eyes to see what was wrong. The chickens squawked like hens on a chopping block.

The wind slammed the little wagon again. It lifted and then crashed down—*BANG!*—and lifted again. The wagon seemed to have no weight at all. Another bounce would surely tip it right over the steep edge of the riverbank, throwing them all into the rushing water.

Rose felt sick to her stomach. The whole world was flying apart.

"Here, take these!" Papa shouted, handing the reins to Mama. He jumped off the seat and ran to the back of the wagon. Rose heard the rope whir as it uncurled over the endgate. The picket pins clinked and the hatchet tapped as Papa drove the pins into the hard ground.

Mama held tight. Her mouth was a thin line in her pale face. Her hands were white. She shouted to the horses over the squalling storm.

"Easy now, don't panic. Whoa! Be still, May! Hold on. Thatagirl, Pet. Steady. Steady, now!"

Rose felt a back wheel settle firmly as Papa

roped it tight to the picket pin. But then the wind tipped the wagon wildly to one side. All the pots and pans crashed one deafening crash.

Finally Rose felt the other wheel settle as Papa tied it off. The wagon felt solid again. Mama got the horses calmed.

Rose looked back to see what Papa was doing. Now the line of wagons waiting for the ferry stretched far, far back, too far to see the end of it. Everywhere was confusion. Babies cried. Children screamed. Horses reared and pawed the air, or ran loose with men trying to catch them. Chickens squawked.

Behind and above, the whole earth rose up in a cloud of dust that curled overhead. The sky had a strange, flat light. Then the sunset turned the huge dust cloud to gold.

"That's your last sight of Dakota," Mama murmured. She said it in such a strange voice that Rose looked at her. She was shocked. Mama's cheeks were damp with tears! Now Rose's throat ached. Her eyes burned. Then, before she could stop herself, she was crying, too. She was afraid, without being sure why.

Papa came back to the front of the wagon. He looked at Mama in wonderment.

"Why, Bess!" he shouted over the wind. "What's the matter?"

Mama handed the reins to Papa. "I'll be all right. In a minute," she said. She pulled out her handkerchief and wiped Rose's face. Then she dabbed her own.

"I'm sorry," she said. "I . . ."

"Now just you never mind," Papa said quickly. "You're tired, is all. You'll feel better when we get across the river, if we can, and get a good hot cup of tea in you."

A few large drops of rain spattered the wagon seat and made dark circles on the dusty backs of the mares.

Rose sniffled and Mama put her arms around her. Rose felt better. But she was still afraid of that river. She hoped they wouldn't cross right away.

In a few minutes the ferry returned. Papa spoke with the ferryman and came back. "It took some persuasion, Bess, but he'll take us across. We have to move fast."

Everything happened quickly. Papa pulled the picket pins. Mama and the ferryman held the colts until Papa could drive the wagon onto the ferry platform. The colts rolled their eyes fearfully and tossed their heads. They pranced skittishly. They had never seen a river or a ferry before.

Papa set the brake and held the lines like iron. The mares braced back on their haunches. The wagon began to skid down the bank.

"Ho, girls! Easy!" Papa shouted.

Their hooves clumped, and the wheels rumbled onto the wooden platform of the ferry. Then the colts came on, standing patiently next to their mothers.

Rose felt a quivery unsteadiness under her, and she grabbed the edge of the wagon seat. But the unsteadiness was the whole ferry. It was tilting and rocking in the water.

Papa stood in front of the mares and spoke to them. Mama made sure the brakes were fast, she checked the chickens, and the ferry began to drift away from the land.

Rose looked back at the shrinking riverbank

and her stomach flip-flopped. Then she looked forward, across the choppy brown waves. She could hardly see the other side. When she looked right and left, all she could see was surging waves of water.

She held on to the seat with all her might, to stop the rocking. She felt as if she might be thrown off at any moment. Her hands ached from holding so tight, but she would not let go for anything.

The ferry pitched this way and that, and the ferryman pulled the dripping guide rope as it slithered past. The ferry skidded sideways and jerked hard against the rope. Rose felt the whole wagon shudder under her.

Foamy waves slapped and slopped all around the ferry's edge, trying to climb onto the wooden planks. The river wanted to tip the ferry over. It pushed with all its might. Only the ferryman's rope kept them from being washed away.

Jagged bolts of lightning slashed the sky, but the rain did not come. Rose shivered, but she was not as scared as before. Mama and

Papa were calm, and the horses stood still. If the horses could be good, so could she.

After many long minutes, she finally saw the far shore looming. She saw the shapes of brushwood trees. Then she could see the light-brown trail at the river's edge, where the road began. But she couldn't see the Cooleys' wagons anywhere.

All in an instant, they landed. The horses' hooves clumped off the ferry deck. The wagon wheels bumped and crunched onto the riverbank.

Rose breathed a quaking sigh. They were safe again, on solid ground. They were in Nebraska.

Mama's Journal

Mama sat in the shade of the wagon, writing about Nebraska.

"The most desolate bare hills I ever saw," she said, dabbing her neck with a handkerchief. "Without houses or fields or trees and hardly any grass."

"I'd just as soon own the whole of it as not," Papa said. "It might do for pasture if it were fenced."

"Well, it reminds me of Lydia Locket's pocket," Mama joked. "Like the rhyme says: 'Nothing in it, nothing on it, only the binding 'round it.'"

The three wagons had stopped early at a small creek, so Mama and Mrs. Cooley could do out a washing. It was hard, hot work. Rose had carried water to boil. Then she stirred the tub of steaming water and clothing with the laundry stick. Mama and Mrs. Cooley hung the scrubbed and rinsed clothes to dry on ropes strung between the wagons. Afterward Mr. and Mrs. Cooley had walked to a farmhouse to buy milk, while Mama had taken out her writing case to write in her journal.

It was Saturday, so they would all take their baths that night. Even when traveling, people stopped to take their Saturday-night baths.

A little way off stood a large camp of many wagons.

Papa sat on the wagon tongue, oiling the harness leather. Rose played fox and geese with Paul and George in the dust under one of their covered wagons. Fox and geese was a game like checkers. They drew the board in the dust, and the pieces were kernels of corn. For the fox to win, he had to capture all the geese by jumping over them. The geese won if they cornered the fox.

Rose had lost all her geese to Paul's fox. So she watched him play George until she was bored. Then she walked over to where Mama was sitting and watched her write. Rose never tired of looking at that case. Papa had covered the slanty surface with lovely soft green felt. At the top of the slanted part he had carved a clever wooden tray where Mama kept her pearl-shaft pen for writing letters. Next to it was an inkwell.

Rose thought of the hundred-dollar bill underneath the green felt surface. She never saw Mama take the hundred-dollar bill out of the case. But she knew it was there, hidden under the envelopes and writing paper.

"Don't forget about the wrong road," Rose reminded Mama.

"That's right," Mama said. "Those boys pointed us toward Crofton this morning, didn't they? We had to turn around and go back to the river and start over on the right road."

Mama licked the point of her pencil. She had spent five cents of her sewing money to buy the little notebook. Almost every day since they left De Smet, she wrote something in it.

"Why are you writing everything down?" Rose asked. "You never did that before."

"No, I didn't," Mama said. "Well, it is like a letter to myself, about our journey. When our trip is over, I'll keep it to remind me."

"I couldn't ever forget the Big Muddy," Rose said.

Mama said she probably wouldn't either. "But small, everyday things are easy to forget," she said. "You will want to remember those things. Life will be changed when you are grown, just the way life has changed since I was a little girl. The wild prairie is tamed now. Big cities are lit by electrified lamps. People can even visit each other from miles apart, simply by talking into a box. The only way to measure our progress is to read about what this country used to be."

Rose wanted to see what Mama had written for that day. Mama handed her the journal. It had blue-lined pages. Where Mama had written in it, the words were small and neat, three lines of writing to each blue line, on both sides of each page. Mama said she wanted that book to last the whole trip.

Rose read:

> *Mr. Cooley got up early and went fishing but did not get a bite. We were all tired from being up so late last night, and did not get started until 9 o'clock. We had taken the wrong road, so we had to go back to the river and start again on the right one.*

"Did you write about the Indian mummy?" Rose asked, flipping through the pages.

Paul and George had finished playing fox and geese. They overheard Rose, and George piped up.

"Mrs. Wilder," he said. "Rose said you used to live around Indians. Did you ever really see any?"

"We lived in Indian Country for a time when I was young," said Mama. "They even came into our house."

"What did they look like?" Paul asked.

Mama's eyes twinkled the way they did when she was telling Rose a story.

"Mama, tell us a story!" Rose begged. "About Indians. Tell us the story about the Indian powwow." That was Rose's favorite. "Please?"

Mama said that story was too long. So she told about the time a wolf pack followed Grandpa home from hunting. Rose had heard that story before, too. But she listened just as intently as Paul and George to Mama's every word. Even Papa stopped rubbing the harness straps to listen. When she got to the end, where Grandpa got home safely, Rose said, "Tell us another. Just one more, please, Mama?"

"Maybe tomorrow," Mama said. "The wash should be dry enough to fold. And I see Mr. and Mrs. Cooley coming with the milk."

Mama closed the writing case. She locked it with the key she kept on a leather cord around her neck.

Mama's journal was like the story of Robinson Crusoe, thought Rose. Only she liked it better because it was real.

Going Swimming

The next day they stayed in the same place. Even when people traveled, Sunday was a day of rest. The horses were picketed out to graze. The trip was hard on them. All day long they pulled the wagons in the heat and dust. They needed a day of rest, too.

Sunday morning after breakfast, Mama read aloud from the Bible: "'Be of the same mind one toward another,'" Mama read from Romans. "'Mind not high things, but condescend to men of low estate. Be not wise in your own conceits.'"

"What's a conceit?"

"It is a way of thinking of oneself," said Mama, "Conceit is vanity—to be full of oneself."

"What does it mean, Come to send to men of low estate?" asked Rose.

Mama laughed. "Con-descend, Rose. Not come to send. It means . . . well, it means to have the same regard for others as you have for yourself."

"Does it say you should like everybody?" Rose had liked almost all the other children in school. But there were boys who were mean to everyone, and she could never like them no matter how hard she tried.

"No one could possibly like everybody they meet," said Mama. "It means to be as kind and generous to friends and neighbors, and even strangers, as you would be to yourself and your family. It is another way of saying 'Do unto others as you would have others do unto you.'"

The sun was blazing, and another day shimmered hot. Mama and Mrs. Cooley sat together on the hammock, having a pleasant talk. Papa helped Mr. Cooley repair a broken harness strap.

Rose explored near the wagons with Paul and George. All across the prairie, the waves of heat bent everything in sight. The wagons in the big camp seemed to be sitting on air. A pale shimmer that looked like water lay in the low places and filled them. That was a mirage.

They broke off some stalks of dried-out wheat and chewed the hard, nutty grains. Rose had to chew a long time before they were soft enough to swallow.

"You could eat wheat all day and still be hungry," Paul said. "But don't swallow any of the seeds whole."

"Why not?" said Rose.

"It might make a wheat stalk grow in your stomach," George said.

Rose tried to remember if she had swallowed any wheat grains without chewing. "You're just teasing," she said.

"It could happen," George said in a serious voice. "A boy in school told me. His pa said the stalk could grow right up your throat and out your mouth."

"That's right," said Paul. "That's why I always spit out my watermelon seeds. Suppose you grew a watermelon in your stomach? How could you ever get rid of it?"

Rose was sure she had swallowed a watermelon seed, at least once. She touched her stomach; it was flat. But after that she was careful to spit out her seeds, just in case Paul and George were telling the truth.

Dinner was cold beans with corn bread Mama had baked the night before. When Rose finished helping with the dishes, Papa had a surprise.

"How would you youngsters like to go swimming?"

"Golly!" Paul shouted.

"Hooray!" yelled George.

"Swimming?" Rose asked. She didn't know how, so she was nervous at first. But when she saw how much Paul and George wanted to go, she decided it might be fun after all.

Mama and Rose and Mrs. Cooley put on

their oldest patched and faded calico dresses over their bare skin. Papa and Mr. Cooley wore just their overalls and shoes. Paul and George wore just their overalls. Country boys and girls never wore shoes in summer—except to church and Sunday dinner, of course.

Rose, Paul, and George raced ahead of the grown-ups to the river. Clouds of grasshoppers flew rustling through the grass ahead of them, then landed with little patting noises that sounded like drops of rain.

The bank of the stream was steep. They held hands to steady each other as they climbed down. The stream was wide, with piles of flat white stones shimmering in the hot sun. The stones were scorching hot to walk on. Between the piles were pools and channels of glittering clear water. It was not muddy and ugly like the Missouri River.

Older boys and grown-ups were swimming in a deep pool in the shade of some trees. The boys were taking turns jumping off a rock.

"Stay close by," Mama said to Rose. "You must not go near the deep water."

"That's right, boys," Mr. Cooley said. "Stay right here."

George looked at Rose, but Paul stared at those shouting, laughing boys and scowled. Soon enough, though, he joined Rose and George in the rippling shallow water.

The sandy bottom was warm, and the sand ran away from under Rose's feet when she walked on it, making her unsteady. When she stood still, the sand drifted over her feet until they were completely covered up.

She was looking at her feet when suddenly water was running all over her head, and then all down her face. It ran down her back and into her dress! The shock took away her breath. Rose just stood there, her arms outstretched.

Then she heard Paul's voice behind her. He was standing there, laughing, with his hat in his hands, water sloshing out of it.

"Golly, Rose!" he shouted. "You're all wet!" He laughed again and threw water from his hat right in Rose's face. She gasped.

For an instant she didn't know what to do.

Then Rose lunged at Paul. She hit him in the chest with both hands, knocking him on his back into the water. Now he was soaking wet, too. He opened his mouth to speak, but nothing came out. His eyes were round with disbelief. He looked so astonished that Rose began to laugh.

Then they all started splashing one another. Paul could throw water on her all the hot day, it felt so good.

They chased one another over the rocks and through the shallow pools. Finally they were breathless. All they could manage to do was sit down in the water.

They took turns pouring hatfuls of water over one another's heads. When it was her turn to get wet, Rose opened her mouth and drank. She wished they could go swimming every day.

Finally it was time to go back to the wagons. Rose was walking ahead of Mama and Papa through the grass when her right foot crunched something on the ground. She held the foot up to see. It was dripping yellow.

"What's that?" Paul asked. He was holding up his foot, and it was dripping yellow, too.

"Look!" George shouted. "Prairie chicken eggs. Their nests are everywhere!"

Now they saw them, hidden in the grass. Hens fled in every direction, and Rose, Paul, and George found the little low nests, full of delicate eggs. Rose took two to show Mama. She could feel the heat from the nesting hen in her palm. "Can I keep them? We could put them under the chickens and see if they hatch."

But Mama said it was a prairie hen's business to raise her chicks. So Rose put the eggs back.

By the time they got to the wagons, the sun had dried their clothing.

At sunset they watched thunderstorms marching across the horizon. The clouds let down dark curtains of rain. Jagged bolts of lightning flickered inside the clouds and stabbed at the ground far away.

That had been a wonderful day. Lying in her bed, Rose realized that now she knew

what an adventure was. It was when something new and unexpected happened. Swimming was an adventure. Even something scary,
like crossing the Big Muddy, was an adventure. She couldn't wait to see what tomorrow's
adventure might be.

The Russians

Each day the three wagons rolled farther south. They began to pass long lines of emigrant wagons coming the opposite direction, heading north.

"Ain't nothin' in Kansas, friend," a man shouted one day from the seat of a passing wagon.

"Where are they going?" Rose asked.

Papa said those people were going to the prairie. They hoped to find a future where Mama and Papa couldn't.

"But why?" Rose asked. "Don't they know about the drought?"

"I reckon they do," Papa said. "But they couldn't find what they were looking for where we're going."

"Well, they must have had bad luck is all," Mama said quickly. "Or made mistakes. There must be some other explanation. After all, no place could be as hard to live in as Dakota."

Lines of wagons came from the east, going west. Other lines of wagons came from the west, going east. Everywhere they met wagons, people asked the same questions: "Where did you come from?" "Where are you going?" "How are the crops up your way?"

Everyone was looking for a better life. But no one knew where it was.

Many wagons were going south to Missouri. The people in those wagons, like Mama and Papa, said they had "Missouri fever."

One day a man in another wagon told Papa and Mama that he had been to Missouri. "We stayed ten days and I'll tell you what: I would not live in Mizzourah if you gave me the whole of it. Why, hardly any of the houses have windows in them, just holes, and lots of the women there have never seen a railroad train nor an organ."

"That's right," the man's wife said. "Ignorant is what those people are. Just plain ignorant."

"And the soil is awful thin and stony," said the husband. "Right there's the place to go if a man wants to bury himself from the world and live on hoecake and clabbered milk."

Mama and Papa drove in silence after that. Rose wanted to know what hoecake and clabbered milk was. But it was time for a little girl to be seen and not heard. For a long while the only sound was the jingle of the harness and the rumble of the wagon wheels. Rose felt like a little mouse, afraid to stir.

Finally Papa spoke. "Well, you can't depend much on the opinion of a man who stays just ten days in a place and then drags his family back to dry country," he said. "He couldn't have seen much in just ten days."

"I expect," said Mama. "There must be another explanation." But her forehead was troubled, and she bit her lower lip.

One afternoon the three wagons camped near a settlement of Russians. None of them had ever seen a Russian before. The Russians all lived near one another in long, low houses made of sod and dried mud that had been whitewashed.

The next day Papa and Mr. Cooley hired themselves out to the Russian farmers. The farmers paid them with potatoes and young ears of corn and cucumbers. Papa and Mr. Cooley even brought back a small pail of milk, with the cream still floating on top.

That night's supper was a feast.

"They live in one end of the house, and the other end is the barn, where the stables are," Papa said.

"It can't smell very good," Mama said, wrinkling her nose. "And it must be noisy."

"It evens up," Papa said. "In a blizzard they don't get lost walking to the barn and freeze to death. The wind can't blow the milk out of the pail, either. They don't need to build barns. There's a saving. And the heat of the animals warms the house. As for cleanliness, Bess, those places sparkle inside and out with white-wash. They look as fresh as new snow."

"Don't get any outlandish ideas, Manly," Mama said. "I've spent enough time in barns to know I wouldn't like to live in one."

Papa chuckled. "The Russians speak only a few English words," he said. "They said their crops were 'nix good this year, nix good last year.' But they are just about the friendliest people you can imagine."

The next day was Sunday. Rose was playing fetch with Ben after breakfast when she looked up and gasped.

"Mama!" she shouted.

Mama looked up from writing in her journal. "Mercy. What is this?" she said. Everyone stopped what they were doing to look. Walking straight toward the camp, across a field, was a large group of people!

"Well, I'll be starched," Papa said. "It's the Russian folks. I wonder what they want."

In a moment they were surrounded by strangers, speaking words that didn't sound to Rose like words at all. There were fathers and mothers, and old people, and more children than Rose could possibly count. Their faces were pink cheeked, their hair was the color of spun gold, and they all smiled warmly.

"Zdrass tvuityeh," one of the women said to Rose. Then she turned to one of the men and said, "Krahseevahyeh, krahseevahyeh."

The men all wore long beards that rested on the fronts of their crisp blue shirts. The boys dressed the same as the men.

The women wore handkerchiefs to cover their heads. Thick braids shining like gilded ropes hung down their backs. The blue of the women's dresses matched the men's shirts, and they wore them over brilliant white blouses with long white sleeves. Their dresses stood out stiff and thick with petticoats. Some wore aprons. The little girls dressed the same as their mothers.

The Russians seemed to be all one family. Rose thought they were beautiful. Just looking at them made her smile. And she loved the mysterious sound of their words. She wondered how they had taught their mouths to make such sounds.

The crowd parted, and two Russian women stepped forward. One of them handed a basket of potatoes to Mama. "Etuh vom padahreck," she said.

The other held out a pail of fresh milk to Mrs. Cooley. The smiling women took a step back and folded their arms in front of them.

"It must be a gift," Mama said.

"I declare," said Mrs. Cooley. "Can you imagine anything so kind?"

"Thank you very much," Mama said to the two women.

"Yes, of course. Thank you," chimed Mrs. Cooley.

"Da. Da," the women said. "Pawzhahlusta."

"Thank you," said Papa and Mr. Cooley.

"Thank you," said Rose.

Paul and George were spellbound. They barely moved their lips.

"The Russians are just curious," said Papa. "They showed us their houses yesterday. I expect they'd like to sit and visit a spell."

For a moment everyone seemed awkward and confused. The Russians did not know what to say. They only smiled and looked around. Finally Mama held out her hand, to show the Russians that they were invited to stay.

"Rose, run and get some grass and sticks," she said. "We'll heat up the stove for tea."

The Russians began to drift about the camp. They looked at the black wagon. They walked around it and pointed, speaking to one another in pleasant voices. Some of the men stood admiring Papa's colts, nodding their heads and pointing.

One of the old bearded men looked at the hammock that Aunt Mary had netted. It was strung between two of the wagons.

"Please," Mama said. "Won't you sit?"

He touched the edge of the hammock and set it swinging.

"Like this," Mama said. She sat down in the hammock and swung back and forth. Then she got up and patted the hammock again.

The old man sat down slowly, awkwardly.

Finally he was in the hammock. He smiled broadly at his friends, leaned back, and in one smooth motion flipped backward, right out of the hammock. He landed in the dust with a thud, upside down with his shoes tangled in the netting.

Everyone was shocked into silence. Then Rose began laughing inside. But the old man looked so funny that her laughter kept growing until finally it burst from her mouth. Then Paul and George burst out laughing, too.

"Rose!" Mama scolded. But Rose could see Mama's eyes twinkling.

Then the old Russian man's belly began to jiggle with laughter. He coughed and said something in Russian. Then all the other Russians laughed, too.

Now all the Russians took turns sitting in the hammock. Some of them fell out on purpose. Then everyone howled with laughter again.

The Russians had an enormous dog with them, taller than Rose. His fur was glossy brown. His clear green eyes and long face made his huge head look like a wolf's. His ears stood up so that they looked like a wolf's ears.

"Mama, the dog is smiling at me."

"Why, yes it is," Mama said. "Even their dogs are sociable."

Rose thought the wolf-dog was the most beautiful dog she had ever seen. He walked right over to her and rubbed against her. He licked Rose's ear with his enormous pink tongue. She wrapped her little arms around his neck and buried her face in his soft coat.

Then Rose felt wriggling behind her. She felt two paws pushing on her back. She turned and there was another wolf-dog! Except this one was a puppy and even more beautiful. The wolf-puppy licked Rose's face, smiled at her, and then wriggled some more. Its bright eyes looked right into Rose's. She gave it a big hug. She fell in love with that puppy. Rose wanted it for her own.

"Oh, Mama," Rose said.

Mama smiled and looked at Papa with raised eyebrows. "Well, Manly?"

Rose's stomach flip-flopped as she watched

Papa turn to one of the Russian men. Papa pointed at the puppy. "That's a handsome pup you have there," Papa said.

The Russian smiled pleasantly and nodded his head. "Da," he said. "Krahseevahyeh."

Papa reached into his pocket and pulled out a coin. He pointed again. "Ahhh," the Russian man said, understanding for the first time. He turned to another man and spoke softly in Russian. The other man nodded his head gravely.

Silently, Rose begged that man with all her might to sell Papa the puppy.

But the Russian turned back to Papa and only shrugged his shoulders.

So Papa pulled out another coin. He jingled the two together in his hand.

The man smiled more broadly and opened his mouth to speak. But just then a little Russian girl rushed over and hugged one of his legs. She buried her face in his pant leg and began to cry. The Russian man put his hand gently on the little girl's head. He spoke to her in a soothing voice.

Then the Russian man looked at Papa and shrugged his shoulders. "Yah izveenyahyus," he said.

"I understand," Papa said, slipping the coins back in his pocket.

Rose felt herself sinking.

"I tried, Rose," Papa said. He squatted by her and scratched the puppy's head. "Looks like a mighty fine dog, too. Maybe we can find another. It seems to be a special Russian breed. Perhaps we will pass other Russian settlements along the way."

Rose couldn't speak without causing herself to cry. She buried her face in the puppy's coat. Then it was time for the Russians to leave. Rose stood up and walked away. The puppy followed her, but the Russian man called out, and it ran back and jumped up on the Russian girl.

All the rest of that day, Rose thought about the puppy. It was almost as if that puppy had been Rose's, and the Russian girl had taken it away. It was wrong to want something that wasn't hers, but Rose couldn't stop herself.

She thought about the beautiful Russians, too, and their wonderful, strange-sounding words.

"Mama, how did the Russians learn that way of talking?" she asked at bedtime. "Who made up those words?"

"Why, the Russians made them up, of course," said Mama. "Russians have been speaking Russian for hundreds and hundreds of years."

"But how did they know? How did they decide the words?"

"I'm sure I don't know," said Mama. "That's a good question, Rose. There are many different ways of speaking in the world besides English. I suppose people who were living near each other a long time ago needed a way to explain things to one another. So they invented words they could all understand."

Rose thought it must be great fun to make up a new way of talking, to think of a horse and invent a brand-new word for it. She tried to think what it must have been like, before there were any words at all.

The Wilders and the Cooleys were about to drive away the next morning when some of the Russians came to say good-bye. The Cooleys were hitched and waiting just down the road. One of the women reached into the front of her blouse and pulled out something that she handed to Mama. Mama was so shocked that she stared at it with a blank face. It was a cold baking of biscuits.

"Gracious . . . goodness," Mama stammered. "Well, how thoughtful. . . . Manly?" she said in a helpless voice.

Those biscuits had been right against that woman's bare skin! Mama's eyes blinked and the color rose in her cheeks. Finally she pulled out her clean white handkerchief and wrapped them up. She smiled politely and nodded her head to show thank you. The Russian woman grabbed Mama and gave her a big hearty hug.

"Oh, my!" said Mama. Rose giggled at the shocked look on Mama's face.

"Ha!" Papa guffawed. Mama glared at him over the Russian woman's shoulder. Papa cleared his throat and covered his mouth with his hand.

Then the Russian woman kissed Mama on both cheeks.

Mama stammered.

Finally the Russian woman patted Mama on the back so heartily that Mama could not have said thank you even if she had known the Russian words. The woman laughed and said, "Dossveedahnyuh."

Mama blushed crimson and touched her hair. She looked at Papa again with pleading eyes.

"I'd say you were quite a success with those folks," Papa teased when they were finally on their way.

"It was not nearly so funny as you would make it seem," Mama said a bit grumpily.

Rose giggled again, remembering the look on Mama's face.

"Now what do we do with these?" She took the biscuits out of the handkerchief. "They came right out of the front of her blouse. I hate to throw food away. But I don't know as I can stomach them."

"They look fine to me," Papa said. "They look clean, and those are clean folks, Bess."

He took one, broke it open, and popped a piece into his mouth.

"Delicious. Light and fluffy," he said, grinning mischievously at Mama. "Give them to the Cooleys and don't tell them. What they don't know won't hurt them."

"I can't do that," said Mama. "What if something was wrong with them? I could never forgive myself. When we stop for dinner, I'll crumble them up and feed them to the chickens."

Kansas

"Look at that, girls," Papa said one afternoon.

"What is it?" asked Mama.

"What?" said Rose.

"Look ahead there," Papa said, clucking to the horses to speed them up. "Can you see it yet?"

Rose saw fields of corn fluttering in the wind. Some cows watched the wagons pass. There was a farmhouse and a barn, and a field of low spread-out trees, set in rows.

Finally Mama cried out, "Oh, Manly! It's an orchard, isn't it? We're in apple country!"

Now Rose saw the small green apples hanging from the branches. "Is this The Land of the Big Red Apple?"

"Not yet, Rose," Papa said, his voice growing lively. "Seems like an orchard holds up pretty well, Bess, even in a drought. Just look at those branches, heavy with fruit! I can't think what could possibly hurt it, now that it's set."

"The orchard gives that farm such a solid, tidy look, doesn't it?" Mama said brightly. A snow-white house and barn sat back from the road, at the edge of the orchard. Rose thought it would be cozy to live in that house, and to pick an apple whenever she wanted.

"And think of all the little songbirds that must live in those trees!" Mama said. "What a lovely place to rest and listen."

"Wait until you girls see an orchard in spring," Papa said. "We had apple trees when I was a boy, in New York state, and nothing beats a field of fruit trees in full blossom."

Seeing that orchard put them all in a wonderful, happy mood. Mama began to whistle.

Then Papa took up the words, and they all sang:

"Old Missus married Will 'the weaver,'
William was a gay deceiver,
Look away! look away! look away!
    Dixie Land,
But when he put his arm around her,
He smiled as fierce as a forty pounder,
Look away! look away! look away!
    Dixie Land.

"I wish I was in Dixie, hooray! hooray!
In Dixie Land I'll take my stand
To live and die in Dixie,
Away, away, away down south in Dixie;
Away, away, away down south in Dixie."

They passed more and more orchards as they crossed the border into Kansas. Day after day the wagons drove through lovely towns with grand houses as big as Rose's school in De Smet. Mama said they were palaces. A high brick fence surrounded one of them.

Granite lions and dogs guarded the gate.

For many miles they crisscrossed the Blue River with its tree-lined banks and its clear, swift-flowing water. Each place they crossed was lovelier than the last.

"Kansas is beautiful," Mama declared one night, putting down her pencil. "If I had been the Indians I would have scalped more white folks before I ever would have left it."

Papa agreed. "I can't think what those folks in Nebraska were talking about. Nothing in Kansas, indeed. I've never seen such corn-fields."

The road threaded its way through rolling hills covered with dark leafy cornstalks. The crops crowded the roadside in places and stretched away in neat rows as far as they could see. But the wind was hot and hard, just like Nebraska. Inches of fine dust lay in the wagon tracks.

"It looks good now," a farmer told Papa. "But the heat and drought made it tassel too quick. I'll be lucky to get nubbins out of it."

In other places, rows of tall thorny trees

grew by the road, thick as walls, keeping half the road in shade. One night they camped by a grove of those trees. Rose heard a man from another wagon tell his son they were Osage oranges.

"The Indians made bows from the heart-wood," the man said. "Farmers plant them in hedgerows, to make a natural fence of the thorns."

Oranges! Rose couldn't wait to tell Paul. She had eaten only three oranges in her life. They grew far away from South Dakota.

"Guess what!" Rose announced. "Those are orange trees over there."

"Oranges?" Paul and George said in amazement.

"Christmas oranges?" Paul said. "Like the kind in your stocking?"

"I don't know," said Rose. "But a man said those are a kind of orange tree."

The three of them explored the dense spiny trees. Sure enough, they found knobby balls, about the size of oranges, hanging from the branches.

"But they're green," said George. "Oranges are orange."

Paul tried to pick one. "Ow!" he howled. "Those thorns are wicked!" Finally he got it. He turned the fruit in his hand.

"Maybe you could just eat it," Rose said. Paul tested the rind with his teeth, but it was too hard to bite into. He got a rock and smashed it open. They each took a piece of the sticky, greenish-white meat to look at and smell. Rose touched hers to the tip of her tongue. Then Paul and George did, too.

"It's awful," said Rose. It left a horridly bitter taste in her mouth.

"Must not be ripe, whatever it is," Paul said with a disappointed frown. They spit out the bad taste and threw away the pieces.

But Rose wasn't discouraged that the Osage orange tasted bad. Anything she did with Paul and George was fun. Rose could hardly remember when she had been happier than she was living on the trail, in the little black wagon.

But the very next night, something happened that changed Rose's feelings. A cool, re-freshing wind had blown away the day's smothering heat. A million stars freckled the clear, sweeping sky. Mr. Cooley built a camp-fire and both families gathered around it to sing hymns before bedtime.

Rose sat on one of the wagon tongues, next to Paul and George. Paul was teasing George by bumping him. Paul bumped him so hard one time that George slipped off the wagon tongue and fell to the ground.

"George, be still," Mr. Cooley said.

George dusted himself off and sat back down on the tongue. He gave Paul a cross look and elbowed him in the ribs. Rose had to stifle a giggle.

When they had tired of singing, Mrs. Cooley said, "I napped so long today, I wonder that I'll ever be able to sleep tonight."

"When I was a sprout, my father often read the Bible to us children on Sunday," Papa said. "It was soothing, and," he added with a chuckle, "it always put my brother and me to sleep."

"Good idea," Mr. Cooley said. "Why don't you read to us, Wilder? I enjoy a good Scripture reading now and then."

"Do read, Mr. Wilder," Mrs. Cooley pleaded.

"Not me," said Papa. "That's my wife's fancy. What do you say, Bess?"

Mama blushed shyly, but all the grown-ups insisted. "Well, there are the last few chapters in Hebrews that I like so well," she said. Mama fetched the Bible from the wagon, lit a lamp to see by, and sat down to read. "'Faith is substance of things hoped for,'" she read, "'the evidence of things not seen.'"

Everyone sat very still, listening to Mama's clear, colorful voice—except Paul. He squirmed and sighed. He kicked his feet in the grass, which made the wagon tongue bounce and squeak.

"Stop that, Paul," Mr. Cooley said, frowning fiercely. Paul stopped. But then he picked a blade of grass to play with. Rose watched as he reached behind George and tickled George's neck. George rubbed his neck as if brushing away a fly. Rose had to stifle another giggle.

Then Paul tickled George's ear. George saw him do it and angrily pushed Paul. Paul pushed back and George nearly fell to the ground again.

"You boys be still now, or I'll wear you out," Mr. Cooley snapped. "Excuse me, Mrs. Wilder."

Mama looked at Rose with a raised eyebrow: She must be quiet as well. Then Mama continued reading. But just knowing she had to be still made Rose feel restless.

She stared into the campfire. She examined her feet and picked a scab on her big toe. She drew a circle in the dust with her foot. Then she watched an ant dragging a large crumb through the grass.

From the corner of her eye, Rose noticed something. Paul was grinning slyly. He lifted his hands and twisted them together. Then he held them up in the firelight. Behind him Rose saw the shadow of his hands on the wagon's footboard. It was a long-eared rabbit. The rabbit wiggled its ears. It opened its mouth and nibbled.

Rose clapped a hand over her mouth to squelch a giggle. Paul winked. He changed his hands. Now on the footboard was the shadow of a wolf, with long ears and a long nose. The wolf shadow opened its mouth, and Paul whispered a howl in Rose's ear, *"Ow-ooooh!"*

Rose could not contain herself a moment longer. She laughed loudly, right in the middle of a pause in Mama's reading.

"Rose!" Mama said.

Rose's face blazed with embarrassment. But she couldn't help giggling. "I'm sorry, Mama," she said. "I couldn't help it! Paul made me."

Mr. Cooley took two great strides toward Paul. His powerful hand swooped down and grabbed Paul's shoulder. Mr. Cooley lifted Paul off the wagon tongue. Paul winced, and Rose winced for him, rubbing her same shoulder.

"Wait, Papa, I . . ." Paul began to speak. But then he fell silent. Mr. Cooley dragged Paul away, behind their wagon.

"Oh, John," Mrs. Cooley said. "Must you?

The boy's a little restless, is all."

"He ought to know by now, Emma," Mr. Cooley grumbled, taking off his belt. "When I say be still, I mean be still."

Tears flooded Rose's eyes. "Mama, Mama, I . . ." The words snagged on a lump in her throat. She hadn't meant to blame Paul. It was only that the wolf shadow made her laugh out loud.

"Hush, Rose," Mama ordered.

Now, even if she could have, Rose dared not speak. She and George sat there on the wagon tongue, cold and stiff, listening to the sound of Paul's punishment.

Mama and Mrs. Cooley sat still as statues. Papa coughed and stared at his shoes. No one said or did anything.

Finally they all heard Mr. Cooley say, "Now get on back there and behave yourself."

Rose bent over and stared at the ground as Mama began to read again. She felt the wagon tongue dip as Paul sat on the far end. Her eyes could not see through the blur of tears that hung in them.

That night as she lay in bed waiting for sleep, tears trickled down the sides of her face.

"Are you awake?" Mama whispered in the darkness.

"Yes," Rose sniffled.

The wagon creaked as Mama got out of bed and sat on the wagon seat next to Rose. A sliver of pale moonlight fell between the edges of the curtains, lighting Mama's face.

"Here," Mama said gently. "Hold out your hand." Rose felt a handkerchief. "Blow your nose."

Rose wiped her eyes and then blew her nose. "Paul didn't do anything wrong, Mama. He didn't, really. I just laughed. I couldn't help it. It was the wolf shadow." The words tumbled out between the sniffles.

"I understand, Rose," Mama said gently. "But there's nothing to be done about it now. You knew it was time to be still. And Paul knows well enough that his father won't stand for disobedience."

"But P-Paul won't like me anymore," Rose hiccuped.

"Paul is not a baby," said Mama. "He knows it wasn't your aim to get him punished."

Mama reached out in the dark and hugged Rose. "Now go to sleep. You will feel better in the morning."

Rose lay in the dark, her thoughts jumping about like jackrabbits. She thought of Paul lying in the dark of his wagon, hating her. She knew she would not feel better in the morning.

A Great City

The horses trudged across Kansas, mile upon dusty mile, sunrise to sunset, day after day. Nothing changed. Yet everything was different. Paul did not speak to Rose. He wouldn't even look at her. So she did not ask to ride with him and George anymore, and they did not invite Rose to play fox and geese. Rose kept herself to herself.

They drove by a fence tangled with blossoming vines. "Look at those lovely morning glories," Mama said. The white flowers formed little trumpets with blushing throats deep enough to hide the bees butting in

134

them. They were beautiful, but Rose only sighed.

"You're as broody as a setting hen lately," Mama said. "Do you feel ill?" She pressed a cool hand to Rose's forehead.

"No," Rose answered.

"Are you homesick?"

"No," said Rose. "Maybe a little. I dreamed about Aunt Mary last night."

"I miss the folks at home myself, now and then," Mama said with a sigh. "But the days are so filled up with new sights and with making camp, cooking, washing, and packing . . . why, I scarcely have a second to think about it!"

Rose didn't want to be broody, but she couldn't help it. She was lonely for the way things were before. She was also tired of the bitter taste of dust. She was sore from sitting and jolting on the hard seat all day. But what cannot be cured must be endured, Rose thought. Everyone was tired of dust. Everyone's bottom ached.

"This sulking won't do," Mama said cheerfully. "I think we need a bit of music. What will it be, Rose?"

Rose shrugged.

"All right, then," Mama said. "I will start." She began to sing in her high, sweet voice. Papa's deep voice quickly joined in. Rose listened to the happy sound of their voices weaving themselves together.

> *"There's a low green valley on the old*
>   *Kentucky shore,*
> *Where I've whiled many happy hours away,*
> *A-sitting and a-singing by the little cottage*
>   *door*
> *Where lived my darling Nelly Gray."*

"Something with a little spark to it, Bess," Papa requested, tapping a foot on the dashboard.

This time they sang,

> *"We'll rally round the flag, boys,*
> *We'll rally once again,*
> *Shouting the battle cry of Freedom!"*

Rose felt her spirits lifting. She hummed along to the next song, which was "Oh, Susanna."

Then they all tapped their feet as Mama and Papa sang,

> *"Oh, drive dull care away*
> *And do the best you can,*
> *Put your shoulder to the wheel*
> *Is the motto for every man.*

> *"Then drive dull care away*
> *For weeping is but sorrow,*
> *If things are wrong today*
> *There's another day tomorrow."*

Rose surprised herself by grinning.

"That's my prairie Rose," Papa said, reflecting her grin. "I was worried you had lost your smile, and we'd have to go back for it."

They were passing two cows grazing by the road. Rose listened to their bells clanging merrily with each tug of grass. One cow's bell was deep: *clang, clang, clang* it rang. Then there was a pause, then *clang, clang, clang* again. The other cow's bell had a higher voice. It rang once loudly, *DING!* followed by two short notes, *ding-ding.*

Those bells made a song: *clang, clang, clang, DING! ding-ding.* Suddenly Rose shrieked, "They're playing it! The cows are playing 'Ta-ra-ra-boom-de-ay'! Listen!"

"By George, you're right," said Papa. "It's plain as pudding, tones, time, and all."

They laughed uproariously, startling the mares so that they turned their heads. The cows bolted in terror, their tails flying and their bells clattering madly. That started a new wave of laughter.

When they had finally caught their breath, Rose helped Mama and Papa sing the song themselves:

> *"Ta-ra-ra-boom-de-ay!*
> *Ta-ra-ra-boom-de-ay!*
> *Ta-ra-ra-boom-de-ay!*
> *Ta-ra-ra-boom-de-ay!"*

Rose felt much better; she was glad to smile again.

One day the wagons rested by a hotel at the edge of a great city. A man told Papa it was more than two miles to the post office in the center. Papa said the town would be too crowded for the colts to run free. So he tied them to the endgate, and the three wagons drove in.

A parade of sights rolled past Rose's eyes. First there were houses and yards and cemeteries, and then they passed stores, smaller ones at first, then bigger ones. There were many hotels and then a livery stable, some more hotels, and a corral next to a blacksmith shop. All of it was the same city, Topeka. Mama said Topeka was the capital of Kansas.

Along the streets stood very tall poles strung with dozens of wires like spider threads. Those were telephone lines, Papa said. Topeka was an up-to-date town, with every modern convenience.

"Just think, Bess. A fellow can check crop prices or find the right bit for his horse without ever setting foot off his land! Why, the savings in time alone must pay the cost of a telephone, not to mention sparing a man his team."

They drove deeper and deeper into a confusion of tall brick buildings. Rose's neck ached from looking up at them. Some of the buildings had six rows of windows. She read aloud the names painted on them: "Bryant's School of Music; Yost and Watson Grocers; J. S. Greeley Real Estate; Al . . . Al . . . how do you say that one, Mama?"

"Alhambra," Mama told her. "It is a Spanish name."

"Alhambra Bath House."

Some of the big glass windows on those tall buildings had fabric awnings in red and white stripes. Others were striped blue and white. Great awnings like droopy eyelids shaded the sidewalks in front of the shops. The buildings drowsed in the hot sun.

Some had beautiful patterns built into the bricks and elegant columns and arched windows. A man looked out one of those windows and shouted to someone on the sidewalk.

The streets were choked with wagons, buggies, and carriages. Where two streets crossed, a policeman stood making the wagons take turns driving through.

The sidewalks were crowded too. Men in overalls and suits stood outside shops next to stacks of boxes and barrels. A few women, dressed in fine silk dresses and feathered hats, walked arm in arm with men in tall black hats.

The hubbub of voices talking, feet clumping on the sidewalks, horses whooshing and nickering, wagons rattling, and buggy wheels squeaking filled Rose's ears. Her eyes were dazzled. It seemed like an enormous celebration going on, like the Fourth of July. Rose tingled with excitement.

Now the web of wires overhead grew more dense. Suddenly a little one-car train full of people came rushing at them. It rode on rails, right down the middle of the street, with no horses or engine to pull it. The car was attached by a pole to the wires above. Rose gasped to see sparks flying where the pole touched the wire.

"That's an electric streetcar!" Papa marveled. He held the reins tight, talking to the team to calm them. The mares obeyed but tossed their heads nervously. Then, when the streetcar's bell suddenly clanged, Mrs. Cooley's team shied in terror and tried to run away. She had to fight to keep them from dragging the wagon onto the sidewalk.

In the middle of the city, the ground was covered with a soft, dark blanket. When the horses walked on it, you could barely hear their footsteps. The wagon wheels made no sound at all. Everything was quiet and lovely. It didn't seem real.

"It looks like tar," Mama said, peering over the side of the wagon.

"Can't be tar," said Papa. "Tar is sticky."

"Papa, look!" Rose said. "Look at the places where the horses walked."

Their hooves had left dents. But right away the dents began to fill in! Soon the black ground was as smooth as if no horse had ever walked there. The blanket had healed itself!

"It can't be rubber," Papa said. "Rubber is

too costly. We have to stop here for supplies anyway. I'll ask the merchants."

The three wagons pulled up to a store. Papa and Mr. Cooley left to buy feed for the horses. Mama talked with Mrs. Cooley while Rose, Paul, and George waited on the wagon seats. She watched men, wagons, and horses flowing through the street. Two ladies in fine velvet dresses, carrying parasols, came out of a hotel and walked across the street.

Three older girls came around the corner of a building. They were talking and laughing in high, lively voices. They were so beautifully clothed that Rose could not stop looking at them. One wore a dress of red serge trimmed with satin and velvet, and a hat with ostrich feathers on it. As she walked past the wagon, Rose could see her lovely clear face. It seemed to be lighted from within.

Suddenly the girl looked up at Rose. Rose smiled bashfully. A flicker of warmth passed over the girl's beautiful face, but then her expression swiftly turned ugly. Rose was startled. Then the girl turned to her friends, whispered something, and laughed.

Rose pulled her sunbonnet down to hide her face. Her neck burned hot. She stared into the lap of her faded and patched blue calico. She tucked her hands under her legs and looked at her bare feet, streaked with dust. All of a sudden, she felt terribly out of place. She felt everyone was looking at her. Rose wanted to leave Topeka right away.

Finally Papa returned and they drove on. "That stuff on the ground is a new manufactured thing called asphaltum," Papa said. "They say it cost the merchants twenty-five thousand dollars to cover the streets in this part of the city."

Mama gasped. "How could they possibly afford it? They must have been bragging."

"I suppose they save on loss from dust damage to their goods," said Papa. "And a city without dusty, muddy streets would draw trade away from other places. In time that asphaltum could pay for itself."

"But to part with such sums, in hard times like these," Mama said. "I can't imagine such extravagance!"

Papa cleared his throat.

"What's in that package, Manly?"

Papa reached into the pocket of his overalls and pulled out a small paper bag.

"Stick candy!" Rose shouted. Papa held the bag open, and Rose picked a red one and popped an end into her mouth. Peppermint was her favorite candy flavor. Mama took one, too.

"You know the package I mean," Mama said, arching an eyebrow. "The big one you put in the wagon."

"Well now, Bess. That's something I was about to explain," Papa said, clearing his throat again. "You see, a fellow was in that store trying to drum up business for this cooking invention. They call it a fire mat, made of a new patented thing called asbestos."

"You bought one," Mama said calmly.

"It's a tremendous unheard-of thing," Papa said earnestly. "It's like a stove lid. You put one over the hottest part of the fire, and nothing you set on it will ever burn."

Mama turned and looked in the wagon. "That's a mighty big package for a stove lid."

"I figure to sell a few along the way, for a profit. I double my money at ten cents each. I can trade them, too." Papa reached back and pulled one out. It was as round as a small plate, gray, and rough like pasteboard. It was edged with a narrow strip of tin.

"Are you sure about this?" Mama said. "It looks like a match would burn it right up."

"I didn't believe it either," Papa said. "So a bunch of us went out back of the store, to the blacksmith's shop, and got him to blow his fire up full blast. Hot enough to melt horseshoes. This fella stuck one of his asbestos fire mats right in it. It glowed bright red, and everybody started to jeer.

"But then he took it out, and that mat was good as new. To save our lives we couldn't make the thing burn. You put one under a pot and the pot could boil bone dry, but not a potato in it would so much as scorch. Why, every woman alive needs one!"

"When did I ever burn potatoes, I'd like to

know?" asked Mama. "If any man came around hinting that I let my cooking burn, he'd get short shrift, I promise that!"

"Don't you worry, Bess," Papa said, and patted her hand. "When you try it, you'll see. I'll get rid of every one of them."

"I hope so," said Mama. "But ten cents doesn't grow on trees. Not for me, anyway."

Journey's End

One afternoon, they drove past a tall whitewashed post. Mama pulled out Papa's pocket watch.

"It is exactly two twenty-four and three quarters P.M.," she said brightly. "And we are finally in Missouri."

Now they saw groves of trees along all the streambeds and around the farmhouses. Trees lined the streets of the towns.

"Look at those big sturdy oaks, Rose," Papa said. "And there are some hickory trees. That's a good hard furniture wood. That tall one with the sleek leaves is a walnut tree. In a month or so you'll be able to pick the walnuts right off the ground."

The road dipped into lush hollows, climbed over sunny hilltops, and then fell again into cozy valleys. Great gray rocks poked out of the ground. The wagons crossed fast-running streams of clear rippling water.

All one afternoon rain poured down, turning the air clean and sweet. It was the first rain they had driven in, and Papa's oilcloth curtains kept the wagon perfectly dry. The rain refreshed their spirits. Mama began to whistle. It made Rose happy to hear it.

"Is this The Land of the Big Red Apple?" Rose asked.

"Not quite, but soon," Mama said. "This is the beginning of the Ozark Mountains. The Land of the Big Red Apple is in the Ozark Mountains."

Rose felt the excitement growing. Mama was friendlier toward strangers. She and Papa talked about land prices and crops with people they met along the way. One night they shared a watermelon with another traveling family.

Mama even let the strangers cook their supper on her stove.

The road grew steep, and it was stony and rutted. The horses' metal shoes clattered on flat flinty stones that lay everywhere. The land was covered with thick leafy trees and bushes. Every turn of the road brought them a new view of woods and hills.

Even the sky was prettier. It felt so close to the ground that Rose thought she could almost reach up and touch it. The treetops seemed to brush the undersides of the clouds. The distances and hills were bathed in a drowsy blue haze.

"The beauty of it just makes you feel wide awake and alive," Mama said. "It is such a contented-looking land."

"You could almost live on the looks of it," Papa agreed.

They passed grand apple orchards. Children playing in front of cozy farmhouses and farmers working by their barns watched them drive by. Some of those houses and barns were large, made of sawed-wood boards. But there were others made of hewn logs laid on top of each other.

In front of those farms, along the road, wooden fences zigzagged. The fences were made of split logs that had been carefully stacked. Horses trotted up to the fences, swishing their tails, to peer in curiosity at the passing wagons.

In the corners of many of those zigzag fences, fruit grew wild. There were blackberries and seedling peaches. There were plums and cherries. And some luscious-looking fruits that even Mama and Papa had never seen before. All this fruit seemed free for the taking, just ripening, falling off, and going to waste.

"Can we stop and take some?" Rose asked. "Just the ones that fell on the ground?"

"No," Mama said. "We haven't time to stop and ask permission."

Beautiful birds, some of them the brightest blue and others brilliantly red with crests on their heads, flitted between the bushes. Cottontail rabbits, with shorter ears than jackrabbits, bounded away into the thick underbrush with Ben yapping after them. Brown birds that looked like prairie chickens skittered away from the wagon track into the bushes. Squirrels chattered, and the trees quivered with the rasping sounds of countless insects.

There was water every littlest way, in springs and brooks and rushing streams. They stopped at a spring of bubbling water as clear as glass, pouring out of a hole in a ledge of rock. The air was cool there.

The wagons stopped often now, to let the horses rest and drink. Their work was harder, for they had to pull the wagons up the steep hills. Their ribs had begun to stick out.

One day the three wagons crested a ridge, rounded a bend, and drove into a little town nestled in a shallow valley. A white church tower poked above the green treetops.

"This is it," Papa said. "This is Mansfield, Gem City of the Ozarks."

Mr. Cooley's wagons led the way. Papa chirruped to the horses, and he, Mama, and Rose leaned forward for a better view. Railroad tracks ran along their right side, sitting high on an embankment. Then they disappeared behind some large white houses with big yards and shade trees. In the backyards Rose could see chickens and pigs.

A gravel path ran alongside the road. Queen Anne's lace bloomed beside the path, the delicate heads nodding in the gentle breeze.

They drove slowly down that street, past more houses, into the town square. The streets around the square bustled with wagons and people, all flowing toward the depot on the far side. A train whistled, and Rose spotted purple smoke unfurling over the trees. Boxes were being brought onto the platform with scraping, thumping sounds. Beyond the depot, on the other side of the tracks, a flour mill puffed small clouds of steam.

The square was a tidy park surrounded by wooden hitching posts. Teams were tied up all around it, the horses' tails swishing away flies. In the middle of the park, a white bandstand gleamed brightly. Delicate lacy molding decorated the roof and railing. Some children played there, pretending to give speeches.

Rows of buildings faced into the park from the other three sides of the square. "Drugs. H. Coday," read the sign on one building. "Reynolds Bro's Cheap Cash House," said another. There was an opera house, a bank, and a saloon. Men sat in tipped-back chairs in front of the stores, watching the comings and goings.

"Seems to be a thriving little town, doesn't it, Bess?" Papa said. Just then the train whistled hoarsely, and the thundering engine slid into the depot, screeching to a stop.

Rose and Papa looked at Mama, waiting for her to speak. Mama's bright, searching eyes looked at everything. "Yes," she finally said. "Yes, it does. I do believe this is where we stop, Manly."

"And where we start anew," added Papa. He reached behind Rose to squeeze Mama's hand. Snuggled between Mama and Papa, seeing the happiness in their faces, Rose felt safe and contented. Their journey really was at an end. Now her travel-weary eyes looked at Mansfield full of curiosity and hope.

Friends Again

The three wagons camped at the edge of town, in a grove of trees just beyond the last house. Trains passed several times a day, and in the night. Each time their shrieking whistles set Ben and the town dogs howling. The trains made grinding, crashing noises as they arrived and left the depot.

"This is not the quietest place we have camped, is it?" Mrs. Cooley remarked in the morning.

"That racket should be music to your ears, Emma," Mr. Cooley said. "Trains mean

commerce, and with commerce comes pros-
perity."

"I'm sure we'll all get used to it in time,"
Mama said. "After all, we got used to those
howling Dakota winds."

Now that their traveling days were over,
they camped every day as if it were Sunday.
Rose helped Mama string the hammock between two trees. Near the wagon Mama hung
sheets to make a screened place for changing
and for taking baths. The table and chairs
were left out, next to the wagon. After breakfast Mama left the cookstove where it stood.

Papa tied the mares under some trees. They
could rest all day now, eating grass and weeds.

There was no more packing and unpacking.
When Rose finished her breakfast chores,
Mama said she could play. She found a parade
of black ants climbing the trunk of a rough-
barked tree. She followed their trail to a patch
of furry moss. From there she followed it to a
thicket of bushes, then a rocky slope, and a
small hollow full of brown-eyed Susans with
fluttering yellow petals.

The ants had worn a little road in the dust by all their traveling. They were busy and hurried, stopping to touch antennae, without seeming to do anything at all.

The clunk of a metal pail startled Rose. She looked up, into Paul's face.

"We found some grape vines," he said, watching the parade of ants. "Your mama says to come help pick."

He dropped the pail he was carrying on the ground and stalked off. Rose picked it up and followed him.

The vines were gnarled shaggy branches of a bush that had wrapped themselves around the trunk of a big tree. The branches had climbed up into the tree's limbs. The large, heart-shaped leaves covered the whole tree. Vines of leaves hung from the limbs to the ground.

Rose didn't see the grapes at first. But then she saw that Paul and George had climbed up onto the limbs of the tree. They were sitting there, reaching down and lifting up the leaves with one hand and tugging at big clusters of dark blue-purple berries with the other. Those were bunches of grapes.

"Mrs. Cooley and I are going to start a fire for a washing, Rose," said Mama. "Just pick what you can reach. The boys will pick what is on the limbs. And remember to leave the unripe grapes for later."

The air around that tree smelled warm and sweet. A curious bee flew around Rose's head, and she brushed it away. She picked a ripe grape and looked at its smooth dark skin. Then she put it in her mouth and bit. The grape burst cool and sweet on her tongue. In the middle were several tear-shaped seeds.

She ate another grape, and another, and another. Then she remembered the pail and dropped the next grape into it. But she noticed that the skin of it was broken. Its purple juice stained the pail. Rose decided she would keep only perfect grapes. So she ate that one. Then she ate two more with split skins.

Finally she found a perfect grape, smooth and round and plump. She placed it gently in the pail.

Rose felt something whiz past her ear, like a bee. But when she looked around, there was nothing there. She went back to picking. Something hit her on the head. An instant later she heard something fall *plink!* into her pail. A crushed grape had joined the perfect ones there.

Rose looked around her again, and then she looked up. Paul was straddling a limb. He was leaning over, intently picking grapes. Rose thought she saw a twitch in his face, but Paul didn't look at her. He just kept picking. George was sitting on a limb on the other side of the tree trunk. Maybe that grape just fell off one of the bunches, Rose thought.

SPLAT! Something squishy hit Rose on the shoulder—another grape. This time she glared at Paul. He was staring at a cluster of grapes in front of him. But now Rose was certain she saw the quiver of a grin.

She picked a grape and held it over the pail, thinking. She mustn't throw it, she told herself. Mama would be cross. Rose looked around. There was no one to see.

So, as hard as she could, Rose flung that grape up at Paul. It smacked on his overalls. A dark stain marked the spot.

"Say!" Paul shouted. He glared down at her, his face dark and pinched. The hard edge in his voice stunned Rose.

He quickly picked a handful of grapes and looked around. Then he threw them at Rose. She ducked, but the grapes splattered her anyway. She felt the sticky pulp in her hair.

Now Rose picked as fast as she could, until her fist was dripping purple juice. She drew her hand back to throw.

"ROSE!"

Mama's sharp, angry voice boomed out right behind her. Rose's heart skipped a beat. She dropped her hand and let the crushed grapes fall to the ground. She stared at her feet.

"Turn around, Rose," Mama said sternly. Rose turned. Bits of grape slid down her forehead. Her fingers were sticky. She felt a damp spot on her shoulder where a grape had stained her dress, and she noticed another stain on the front.

"Land sakes!" Mama cried out. She clapped a hand over her mouth. A stifled laugh came out, and she turned away. Rose stared at Mama's hem, not knowing what to think.

Finally Mama turned back. She cleared her throat and smoothed her apron.

"You have soiled your dress," she said soberly. "And throwing perfectly good food around is a sin and a waste, Rose. Now get on back to the wagon and clean yourself up. Dampen those stains, too, before they set. Then you can just sit on the wagon seat until I call you to help with dinner. I think you've had enough grapes for today."

Rose frowned at Paul. He grinned at her mockingly from his perch in the tree. Then he stuck his tongue out, wet and purple. Rose spun and stomped off to the wagon. She could hear Paul call out to George, as if nothing had happened. "Over here, George. There's a bunch of ripe ones."

Rose washed her face and hands and rinsed the sticky pulp from her hair. She dipped water from the bucket and poured it on the stains on her dress. Then she rubbed hard. She complained to herself the whole time. It wasn't fair. She hadn't started that grape fight. Paul had tricked her. Now she had to be good while everyone else had fun.

Suddenly Paul peered at her around the end of the wagon.

"Serves you right," he said.

Rose was too surprised to speak.

"Serves you right for telling," Paul went on, walking up to her. "Too bad you're a girl, or you'd get a good licking. Then you and I would really be even, wouldn't we?"

"That's not—" Rose began, but Paul cut her off.

"I don't care about the whipping," he said. "But you tattled. You said I made you laugh. That was just about a lie anyway. It wasn't my fault you couldn't keep quiet."

Paul's blue-black eyes were the color of a thundercloud. His black eyebrows pinched down, and his mouth curled. Rose cringed.

"I wasn't telling," she said. "I didn't mean you *made* me. I only meant the wolf shadow

163

made me laugh."

"Then why didn't you say it?"

"I tried. But Mama wouldn't let me. And I was scared of your pa."

"Pshaw!" Paul snorted. "He's nobody to be scared of. Every boy gets a licking now and again."

"Mama and Papa never even spank me," Rose said. "It must hurt awfully."

"I already told you, it's nothing," said Paul. "I'd just as soon forget about it."

"But why didn't you tell your pa you didn't make me laugh?" Rose asked. "Wouldn't he listen if you—"

"Look here," Paul interrupted. "I don't tattletale on anybody. Not even George. And I wouldn't tell on a girl, even if she lied all day. My pa would thrash the hide off me anyway. So just shut up about it!"

Just then Mrs. Cooley called out Paul's name.

"I better get back to picking," Paul said. He turned to leave, but then he stopped and looked at Rose over his shoulder. He grinned shyly. "I found a place where there are lots of hazelnuts. After dinner, I'm going to go hunt some."

"That would be fun," said Rose, smiling back.

She finished rubbing out the stains, then climbed onto the wagon seat. She sang to herself and laughed at two squirrels chasing each other through the trees. Rose didn't know how it had happened, but Paul had forgiven her.

The Little Dog

Papa rode May out of camp each morning, looking for work. He took some of the asbestos fire mats with him to sell. In the evening Rose and Mama eagerly watched for him to come riding back, to tell them the news.

"Hello, girls!" he called out from the saddle. Then he tied May up, washed his hands, and sat down to eat.

"Saw a place today, but it was too big for us," he said between bites of corn bread and beans. "The land's real stony here. It won't do for growing much oats or wheat. That's why folks got to planting orchards. Used to be all big trees around here. After the timber companies cut them down, they sold the bare land off for farms."

Mama listened with a fierce new light in her eyes. She asked many questions. "What about the town? What about the merchants?" she asked. "Do they appear honest? Is the trade brisk?"

"It has everything we could want, Bess. It's central for shipping cream and eggs, right on the trunk line between Memphis and Kansas City. They ship express to St. Louis, too. The town ought to grow fast."

"Thank goodness," Mama said. "If the hens will just keep laying. How do eggs sell?"

"Twelve cents a dozen."

"It isn't as much as in Dakota," Mama said, frowning. "But then I suppose everything is a bit less here. What about churches?"

"I'm afraid we'll have to do our worshiping without a Congregational church, Bess. There's Methodist and Presbyterian."

"We'll choose once we're settled," said Mama.

———

The next night Papa said, "Saw a real pretty place, Bess. Had its own pond. Most of it already in pasture. You would have liked it well enough. But it's just twenty acres and we haven't any stock to graze. A man can't support a family on that."

Papa saw many farms. Some were just right but too costly. Some were too hilly, or too flat. Some had smooth pastures, but they flooded in the spring. Some farms sat on dry ridges, and water had to be carried a long way.

"We can't look forever, Manly," Mama said. "We must be settled before snow flies."

"Don't you worry," Papa said. "Something will turn up."

Mama and Mrs. Cooley did chores together, sewed, and read. Mr. Cooley also looked for work, and for a home for his family.

Rose played in the woods every day with Paul and George. They were glad to be free of those hard wagon seats and could hardly be still. But they learned right away that the Ozark hills were covered with sharp stones and rocks. Every day they stubbed and cut their toes. Mama wrapped Rose's bruised toes in scraps of old clothing, to keep her from hurting them again.

The woods were full of the good clean smells of the living earth: rotting logs, dusty weeds, and the damp underneaths of last year's oak leaves. They found toadstools growing like little parasols on dead trees, and peeking from under dead leaves. Mosses that looked like the teeny-tiniest forests clung to rocks.

They tasted wild greens after letting the mares sniff and nibble. Mama said not to eat anything the horses refused. They found a bed of clover and gathered every blossom. Then they sucked the sweet juice from the roots of the little petals. They ate dandelion leaves and the bitter stems. They ate the tender leaves of dock and the soft ends of grass stems pulled from the joints.

They climbed trees. At first Rose could not pull herself up. Her arms trembled with the effort. Her feet scrambled for something to stand on. But Papa showed her how to hug a tree trunk. Then Rose could push up with her legs and pull with her arms at the same time.

Soon all three of them were perched in the trees like birds. Rose climbed from one limb to another, higher and higher, until the limbs got too small to hold her. When she looked down, her stomach flip-flopped.

She could see the dusty tops of the wagon covers. The wagons looked much smaller. She could not see the horses' legs under their bodies. Even the long-legged colts looked round and stocky from up there.

The chickens looked like toys. Rose liked teasing them by dropping green acorns on them. They squawked madly and ran as if they had seen a hawk's shadow. Rose giggled.

"I know you're up there," Mama said. "The chickens won't lay as long as you're scaring them half to death."

Mama had no legs at all. Papa was just a hat, walking around the wagons.

Squirrels scolded them from the limbs of other trees. Birds hunted for seeds and insects. The tree bark was alive with ants and moths and soft fuzzy caterpillars, striped brown and black.

At a creek near the camp Rose found strange stones. She found a thin little one in the shape of a triangle. Its edges were wavy all around, and the point of it was sharp enough to cut tree bark.

"That is an Indian arrowhead, I'm sure," Mama said. "Indians lived here a long time ago. They used small stones to make sharp flat points for their hunting arrows."

Rose collected dozens of Indian arrowheads and kept them in a scrap of folded cloth. Paul found a stone that Mr. Cooley said had been an old Indian axhead.

Rose was sifting through stones in the creek one morning when she looked up and saw that a little dog was staring at her. Its short coat was white with black and tan spots. Its pointy ears stood up from its pointy face.

Rose saw right away that the little dog was hungry. Its hip bones and ribs stuck out, and it looked at Rose with big, sad eyes. Its tail hung limp. The sight of it made Rose's heart ache.

They stared at each other without moving for a moment. Then the little dog looked at the water and panted. It laid its ears back and looked from side to side, as if it were about to run away.

"What's the matter?" Rose asked. "Are you thirsty? Go ahead and drink. I won't hurt you."

She dipped the palm of her hand in the water and gave herself a drink, to show that it was all right.

"I won't hurt you," she said again.

The dog's ears pricked up. Then it began to lap up the water in the creek. But it kept its eyes on Rose.

"Stay here," Rose said to the dog. "Don't go away." She ran to the wagon.

"Mama, could I have some corn bread? Could I have a johnnycake, please?"

"It's almost noon, Rose. Dinner will be ready as soon as Papa gets back from town."

"It isn't for me," Rose began, all fidgety. "It's for . . . for somebody else."

"Who?" Mama said, a puzzled look on her

face. "Who could it be for, Rose?"

"For . . . for a little dog. If we don't give it something it might starve."

"Show me this dog," said Mama.

She followed Rose through the woods, down to the creek. The little dog was there, lying by the water. It looked at them with sad eyes.

"The poor thing," Mama said. "Look at it, half starved to death. It must have gotten lost from its wagon."

Rose sat on her heels and talked to the dog while Mama went to get some food. She brought back a little corn bread, and a tin cup with some milk in it. The dog got to its feet and backed away when Mama put the food down. Then it cautiously sniffed at the food and nibbled the corn bread.

"You can stay and watch it eat," Mama said. "I have to finish cooking. I'll whistle when it's time to come help with dinner."

Rose watched the dog eat every last crumb of the bread. It lapped up the milk with its dainty pink tongue. Then it gave itself a little shake and started to walk away.

"Wait!" Rose blurted. The dog stopped and looked at her.

Just then Mama whistled. Rose picked up the tin cup and walked slowly backward, up the hill toward the wagons.

"Come on," she said. "Are you still hungry? I'll give you some more milk. Come on. Come on."

The dog took three steps toward Rose. Then it stopped and looked around. Rose could see it shivering.

"Come on. I won't hurt you. What's your name? Come and see my friends, Paul and George. We won't hurt you."

The dog's tail twitched once. Then it turned and trotted off into the woods.

"Wait!" Rose pleaded. "Come back!"

The little dog stopped again to look back at Rose. Then it kept going until it disappeared.

Rose sighed and trudged back up the hill. Mama was standing at the stove holding her head back from the spattering meat. "Did it eat it up?"

"Yes," Rose said glumly. "But then it went

away. Why didn't it stay, Mama? Why didn't it come with me?"

"Stir the mush while I make gravy," said Mama. "Perhaps it has been mishandled. It may be just as well, Rose. A stray animal could be diseased. It's all skin and bones. But don't fret. In time we'll find ourselves a good dog."

Rose looked out into the woods, but nothing stirred. She hated the thought of that little dog wandering about, hungry and lonely.

A Little House

Papa rode into camp for dinner without saying hello. Rose's eyes met Mama's for a worried moment. He took a long time tethering May, then stopped to stroke Pet. Although Rose and Mama never forgot, he checked the pails to make sure the horses had water.

He washed his hands at the bucket by the wagon without a word. But he looked at Rose for an instant, and she saw a twinkle in his eye. Then she stopped worrying. Papa never looked excited when he really was. Instead, he became calm and quiet.

Mama knew it too. She set the bowls of food on the camp table. Then she waited, arms folded, staring at Papa while he rinsed his hands and dried them carefully on the towel. Then he wet his hair and mustache, and combed them neatly. Finally, he sat down and waited for Mama to say the grace.

That was the shortest grace Rose had ever heard. She barely had time to close her eyes before Mama finished: "Thank-thee-Lord-for-the-bounty-we-are-about-to-receive-Amen. For heaven's sake, Manly! What is it? Have you found a farm?"

"In fact, I believe I have," Papa said quietly, pushing beans onto his fork with a piece of corn bread. "We can see it, soon as dinner is over."

There had never been a faster dinner. Rose was still eating when Mama got up to change into her best calico. She was in such a hurry, she put the buttons in the wrong holes. When Mama was excited, anyone would know it.

Papa saddled up the mares.

"You stay in camp and mind Mrs. Cooley

while we're gone," Mama said. Then Pet and May carried her and Papa out of sight.

They were gone all afternoon. Rose had never known such a long afternoon. She played fox and geese with Paul and George, but she kept losing. Every little while she dashed down the hill, to see if the dog had come back to the creek. But it was nowhere to be seen. The rest of the time she listened for Mama and Papa returning.

At last, after Mrs. Cooley had begun to cook supper, Rose heard Mama whistling as she and Papa rode into camp. Papa's eyes glowed. Mama's whole face was shining. Rose had never heard her talk so fast.

"Just what we wanted," she told Mrs. Cooley. "So much, much more than we'd hoped for. It has a year-round spring of the best water you ever drank. There's a log house, in woods, on a hill, just a mile and a half from town. Rose will be able to walk to school! It's a little house, but I have always lived in little houses. I like them.

"And, just think, to cap it off, a thousand

young apple trees, in nursery rows, just waiting to be planted as soon as we can clear the land."

"Apple trees?" Rose asked excitedly. "Are we going to have apples?"

But the grown-ups were too busy chattering to notice her. Paul and George looked at Rose with big eyes.

"It's a modest place," Papa told Mr. Cooley. "Sits on several rocky, brushy ridges. That's why it's only ten dollars an acre. I confess I know nothing about apple trees. The fellow who owned it bought the trees, and then he ran out of money.

"But the timber's in fine shape. You can see the place could be profitable, if we can hold out till the trees bear fruit."

Finally Mama said to Rose, "How would you like to live in a little house—a log cabin in the woods—like I did when I was a little girl?"

"Are we going to have apple trees?"

"Apple trees, and more water than we can ever use, and all the wood we could ever burn." Mama's voice was light and cheerful.

They talked about that farm until it was past everyone's bedtime. Mama said they would talk to the banker about the farm in the morning.

Rose woke from a bad dream: A growling animal had been chasing her through the woods. She lay in bed, trying to remember it. Outside the wagon, the forest was cloaked in darkness and perfectly still, listening to itself. No wind stirred the trees. Even the insects had gone to sleep. In the distance a train wailed mournfully.

Suddenly Rose heard a real growl! It came from right under the wagon. She sat straight up.

"All right now. Easy there," a man's voice said. "Wilder!" the voice called out. "Wake up!"

Rose peeked through the corner of the curtain. It was Mr. Cooley, carrying a lantern. He had come to get Papa for morning chores. Rose heard another growl.

Papa stuck his head out the other end of the wagon. "What is it, Cooley?"

"Don't you know?" Mr. Cooley said. "There's a runt of a dog under the wagon. Acts like he wants a taste of my leg."

"A dog?" Rose shouted.

Papa climbed out of the wagon to look.

"What in tarnation?" Papa said.

Rose climbed down the wagon wheel and looked. In the wavering light of the lantern sat the hungry white dog with the black and tan spots.

"It's him, the one I told you about, Papa!" Rose shouted. "He came back."

The dog walked over to Rose and sat down. Rose scratched his head, and his dark eyes gleamed up at her in the light. She stroked his short fur, feeling the hard muscles underneath, and the bones. Rose just had to hug him. He gave her face a little lick.

"Seems the little feist has adopted us," Papa said, scratching his head. "Every farm needs a good watchdog. Shall we keep him?"

"Yes!" Rose shouted. She hugged the dog again, and he wriggled in her arms. His tail slapped the leaves.

They all got dressed and Mama made breakfast. But first, she gave the little dog some more corn bread and milk, and some cold beans.

"It's the least we can do," Mama said. "He certainly has proven his loyalty."

The children all watched the little dog eat.

"Even if he were all filled out, I bet one of your best hens would outweigh him, Bess," Papa said.

"He's no prize," Mrs. Cooley agreed. "But he sure is lovable."

"Maybe he belongs somewhere," said Paul.

"He looks like he's been on his own for some time," Mr. Cooley said. "Probably trying to keep up with an emigrant wagon."

Rose could see the little dog wasn't beautiful like the Russians' wolf-dog. He was small and fragile-looking. His spindly legs trembled and his eyes were sad. But Rose didn't care. There was something about that dog.

"I'm going to take the very best care of you," she told him. He pricked up his ears and looked at her. "I'll never let you go hungry again."

Mama, Papa, and Rose shared little bits of their breakfast with him. He ate everything right up, licked their hands in thanks, then lay down next to the wagon wheel.

Rose watched him the whole time she helped with the dishes. He was lying down, but his ears were awake, turning this way and that to the sounds of the camp.

"What should we call him?" Rose wondered.

"He might have a name, but we would never learn it," said Mama. "We'll think of a new name."

"How about Jack?" Rose said. "You like the name Jack for a dog."

"He's no Jack," said Mama. "He needs his own name. Now, what's a good name for a faithful watchdog? How about . . . Fido?"

"Fido? What's a Fido?"

"That is a very old Latin word. It means faithful and loyal."

"Fido," said Rose. The little dog's ears perked up. "Fido," she said again, a little louder. The dog raised his head, looked at

Rose, blinked and panted.

"He smiled at me!" Rose shouted "He knows we are talking about him. Fido knows."

Then she said it again, "Fido," just to hear it one more time. Yes, she decided. Fido was a perfect name.

Lost!

Rose sat on a stump next to the wagon, watching Mama brush and braid her hair. Papa lathered his face at the washbasin, set on the folding table. Then he began to shave. Mama and Papa were going to town to see the banker.

"What's a banker?" Rose asked.

"A banker lends money," Mama said. "He is lending us money to buy the farm."

"But what about—" Rose stopped before she said another word. She remembered she must never mention the hundred-dollar bill in the writing case.

"That isn't enough to buy a farm," Mama said, knowing what Rose was going to say. "The banker lends the rest."

She brushed her thick, roan-brown hair in sweeping strokes. Mama's hair was so long that even when it was tightly braided, she could sit on the braid. Rose loved the silky, smooth feel of it right after Mama brushed it out. It slipped through her fingers like water.

Mama was the most beautiful of her sisters. Everyone said that. Rose thought Mama was most beautiful in the morning, when her hair fell over her back, with the light racing through it. But she always wove it into one wide braid. For dressing up she wound the braid into a big, tight bun on the back of her head. She fastened it in place with tortoise-shell pins.

"It's pretty when the braid hangs down," Rose said. "Can't you leave it like that?"

"It isn't a ladylike way to wear it," Mama said. "A woman can't go to town looking as if she just came from feeding the chickens."

Fido leaned against Rose's leg. They

watched Mama fluff her bangs into a soft little mat on her forehead. She checked herself in the looking glass that hung from a tree branch. All the while she whistled "Oh, Susanna."

Then Mama buttoned her shoes with the buttonhook and went to the wagon. She got out a large pasteboard box, and Rose followed her behind the hanging sheets of the changing place. Mama took off her calico dress and folded it neatly. Standing in her bleached-muslin petticoats and her corset trimmed with lace, she opened the box and took out her best dress. It was the black cashmere that she had worn to marry Papa. Rose had not seen it since that long-ago night when they had said good-bye in South Dakota.

Mama squeezed her arms into the tight sleeves of the basque. She carefully buttoned all the glittery jet buttons up to her chin. Then Rose helped her center the points of the basque exactly in the middle.

Rose handed Mama her gold bar pin, which had a little house and lake etched on the surface. Papa had given it to Mama the Christmas before they were married. Mama pinned a bit of ribbon, the color of robin's egg, to the front of the stand-up collar. Then she pinned on her black sailor hat, with the blue ribbon around the crown. It had a spray of wheat standing straight up at one side.

Her braided bun tilted the hat forward just a little, giving Mama a jaunty look. The narrow brim rested on the curls on her forehead.

The last thing she did was pull on her brown kid gloves. Rose thought Mama had never looked more beautiful.

When she came out from the dressing place, Papa just stared at her for the longest moment. His eyes had a soft look in them.

"Look at the time," Mama said, touching her hair. "You had best shake a leg, Manly. We don't want to keep Mr. Freeman waiting."

Papa chuckled and went to the screened place to change his shirt. Then he combed his hair and mustache and put on his best hat.

Mama took out a clean handkerchief and spread it on the table. Then she laid on it her little red cloth pocketbook with mother-of-pearl sides. Rose knelt on one of the chairs and leaned her elbows on the table.

Mama whistled "Yankee Doddle" as she went to the wagon and brought back the writing case. She set it on the table, unlocked it, and opened it. She lifted the felt-covered lid of the compartment where she kept her writing paper and envelopes.

Mama lifted the paper and envelopes. She looked underneath. Then she stopped whistling. She drew a sharp breath. The light in her face went out, all in an instant. She quickly opened the lid of the other compartment. She peered inside it. Her jaw sagged and her forehead knotted up.

Rose shrank from the sight of Mama's face.

Papa came and looked over Mama's shoulder. Mama turned to him with pleading eyes.

"Can't be," he said calmly.

The hundred-dollar bill was missing!

Everything changed in that moment. To look at the expression on Mama's face gave Rose a terrible sinking feeling, like stepping in a hole she didn't know was there.

"I last saw it in Fort Scott, in Kansas," Mama said. "When I wrote the folks in Dakota." She began rustling through everything in the case. She shook every sheet of writing paper and laid them all out on the table. She looked inside every envelope. She took every letter she had gotten and saved out of its envelope and unfolded it. She looked into the empty envelopes and shook them out.

Then Papa took out the ink bottle and pen and turned the whole case upside down. He shook it so the hinged lids swung in the air. But nothing more came out.

Mama and Papa sat down. Papa twisted an end of his mustache. Mama twisted her handkerchief. Rose sat perfectly still, afraid to move.

"This simply cannot be," Mama said. "We must be losing our senses." Then she looked at Rose. Her face was pinched.

"Did you maybe tell someone, Rose? Even just accidentally, without meaning to?"

"No," Rose said softly. Mama had said it was a secret, and Rose had kept it.

Now Papa looked at her too. "Did you ever see a stranger near the wagon when we weren't here?" he asked. "Did you see any strangers in the camp?"

"No." Her eyes began to sting.

"It must be here, Bess," said Papa matter-of-factly. "Where else could it be?"

They sat there still and silent for the longest time. They stared at that case as if it might begin to speak at any moment, as if it might tell them where the hundred-dollar bill had gone.

Rose heard the murmur of Paul and George's voices on the other side of their wagons. The leaves rattled and whispered in the trees overhead. The insects thrummed all around them. But the writing desk just sat there, empty and silent.

"Well," Mama finally said. Rose knew what Mama meant: What cannot be cured, must be endured. Mama peeled off her gloves. She turned them right side out, finger by finger, and smoothed them on the tabletop.

"You may as well go explain to the banker, Manly," she said. Her eyes shimmered with tears, but her voice was steady.

"Now don't go blaming yourself, Bess," Papa said gently. He put a hand on her shoulder. "We aren't licked by a long sight. We've always managed. Something will turn up."

"You know as well as I do: Nothing turns up that you don't turn up yourself," Mama said. "Perhaps this will prove providential in some way, but I can't see how. We came so far, and we were so close." She bit her lip.

"Don't forget, we still have the colts," said Papa. "You know how folks admire them everywhere we go. Even with things being as bad as they are, anybody would give a hundred and twenty-five for Prince without batting an eye."

"No, Manly!" Mama cried out. "Prince is your colt. If we must sell one of the colts, sell mine. Little Pet isn't as sturdy as Prince, and I'll be too busy on the farm to break her anyway."

"Let's not get ourselves too far down the road," Papa said. "We need to think on this a spell."

Rose's heart sank. She loved Little Pet and Prince like family. Her throat ached at the thought of either one being led away by a stranger.

"Rose, you may run and play now," Papa said.

But Rose didn't feel playful. She wanted to be by herself and think. She walked into the woods, with Fido prancing alongside. He didn't know about the hundred-dollar bill, or the colts. He was only grateful for Rose's company. She stooped to scratch his head. A tear ran down her cheek and splashed on Fido's nose. He gave Rose's cheek a lick.

For that moment, Rose wished she could be Fido instead of herself.

A Wonderful Discovery

W hatever will you do?" Mrs. Cooley asked at supper.

"We think it best to take our time deciding," Mama said pleasantly, but her voice was solemn. "What will you folks do?" she asked.

"My farming days are over," Mr. Cooley said. "I'll sell the second wagon and team. That will put a roof over our heads till I find steady work in town. I'm tired of fighting the land just to keep storekeepers and bankers in silk stockings."

"I guess we will always be farmers," Mama

said with a sigh. "What's bred in the bone never will come out of the flesh. Town life doesn't agree with me. It's so peaceful in the country. That little farm was just . . ." But she stopped herself from saying more.

No one knew what to say. Rose cast a worried look at the colts.

"We can hold out so long as the weather does," Papa finally said. "It's a blessing to be this far south, anyway. Here it is September and still warm and green as summer."

For some days Papa loaded boxcars at the depot. That was hard work. He was so tired after supper that he climbed into the wagon and fell right to sleep.

One day he packed apples and brought back a sack of them, sweet and juicy. Both families sat around the campfire eating crisp, tangy apples. Papa let Rose feed the cores to the horses.

The next morning, while Papa was feeding the horses, Mama whispered to Rose, "I have a surprise for Papa. Don't say anything until we eat."

Mama put salt pork on to fry. She said Rose could help slice up some onions, nice and thin. Rose knew how to peel and slice potatoes and apples, but she was still learning how to use a knife for other things. Onions were slippery. It was hard to make the slices even. The onion juice made Rose's eyes tear. She rubbed them with her hands, but that only made them burn. They stung so that Rose nearly cried.

"Go splash water on your face," Mama said, wiping Rose's teary eyes with the hem of her apron. "I'll finish the onions. You can help with the apples."

When the meat was cooked, Mama put it on the platter to drain. Then she laid the onion slices in the bubbling hot drippings. She cored apples and Rose helped slice them, with the red skin still on.

When the onions began to brown and smelled deliciously sweet, Mama laid the apple slices on top. Then, over all of it, she sprinkled brown sugar. The smell of the apples and onions frying together made Rose's mouth water.

Finally Papa finished his chores. He washed his hands in the bucket and came to the table. Mama had covered the platter with a cloth. She brought it to the table and set it down. Then she snatched away the cloth with a flourish. Steam rose in the cool morning air from the golden brown stack of onions and apples and fried salt pork.

A wide, happy smile spread across Papa's face, crinkling the laugh lines around his eyes. He took a deep sniff and sighed with contentment.

"You're the cat's whiskers," he said. "My favorite dish—fried apples'n'onions."

"I helped!" Rose shouted. Papa got up and gave Mama a hug.

"Manly, really!" Mama said, blushing.

Then Papa gave Rose a brushy kiss.

"Thank you, girls," he said. "We haven't much, but sometimes I think there isn't another thing in the world I'd lift a finger to take."

When Papa said that, Rose knew everything would be all right.

They were so hungry, they ate everything. There weren't even any scraps left over to give Fido.

"What will he eat?" Rose asked Mama.

"He's getting his strength back, and he's a resourceful dog," said Mama. "I saw him catch a mouse yesterday. Fido won't starve."

At dinner Rose left some beans on her plate, to scrape for Fido. But Mama scolded her for wasting food. Then Rose let Fido lick the empty plates. But Mama said that was unhealthy.

After that Rose sneaked food from her plate when Mama and Papa weren't looking. She hid crumbs of corn bread in the folds of her dress. She carefully held her hand against her leg when she stood, so the crumbs wouldn't fall.

Behind the wagon she knelt and let the crumbs drop on the ground. Fido gobbled them up, his tail wagging gratefully.

When Mama wasn't looking, Rose also let him lick her empty plate.

———

One day Mr. Cooley hitched up his second team and drove away his second wagon. He had sold it.

A man from the livery stable came to look at the colts. When he left, Papa said the man had made a fair offer for Little Pet. "It's enough to get a mortgage on the farm, Bess. And Freeman, the banker, says it's still for sale."

Rose's stomach bunched up in a knot.

"It would be hard to let Little Pet go," said Mama thoughtfully. "But I can't see another way. If we don't buy a farm, how will we live? Once the harvests are in, there won't be any work for hire until spring plowing. The horses need room to graze. The hens need shelter."

"But, Mama . . ." Rose began. Then she realized she had interrupted.

"You must remember what is important, Rose," said Papa. "Winter is coming. You and Mama and I need a home. All the horses will surely go hungry if Little Pet stays. But if someone buys her, she is such a fine colt, they will feed and brush her every day, and give her a warm bed of clean straw every night. Then the mares and Prince will have more to eat. We will all be better off."

"Yes, Papa," Rose said softly.

"Don't you worry about this now," he said, sitting in a chair and pulling Rose onto his lap. He nuzzled her cheek. "Your mama and papa have been through far worse scrapes, and look at us now!"

The next day Mama did a washing. Rose was stirring the pot when Paul came running, calling to Rose, "We're moving into town! We're going to live in the *hotel*." His eyes were wide with excitement. "My folks are going to run it. George and I are going to help. Gee willikins, Rose. It's so exciting!"

Rose had never been in a hotel, although they had driven past many. Mama had told Rose that hotels were not places where children went, which made hotels wickedly interesting.

"What could you do in a hotel?"

"I can carry bags," Paul said, throwing his head back importantly. "Papa says I can help meet the trains when they come in, and bring the customers." But then he smiled like a boy again. "Golly, Rose. I like it so much better here than in South Dakota!"

The glow on Paul's face lifted Rose's spirits. She liked it better here too. But she thought about the Cooley's loading their wagon and driving out of camp. Then she felt sad. That night the forest whispered lonely sounds to her. The crickets chirped mournfully in the cool autumn air.

The grapes were almost gone now. But the next day Mama and Rose found one last vine that still had clusters the birds and bees hadn't picked over. They collected a pailful.

Rose sat at the table sorting out the spoiled ones while Mama wrote to Grandma and Grandpa. Rose didn't eat a single one. They needed them all to make a pie. Mama said they were so juicy, she would have to thicken them first.

"I never heard of grape pie," Rose said.

"Neither did I," said Mama. "But we don't have enough sugar to make jam."

Rose held up a wrinkled grape for Mama to see. "This one?"

"That one is good," said Mama. "Now, what

shall we tell Grandma and Grandpa? The weather has been clear and dry. Very pleasant, really."

Mama's pen scratched across the page, dipped into the inkwell of the writing case, and scratched some more. Rose put the pie grapes in a bowl on the table. She set the bad ones aside, to feed to the horses.

The rich brown wood of the writing case was so shiny that Rose could see a reflection of the bowl. Along the bottom of the case was a thin crack, where Papa had attached the sides. Something white was in there, in that seam. A speck of white. Rose picked at it with a fingernail.

"Don't do that, Rose. It's bothersome when I'm writing."

"Something is stuck there," said Rose. She picked some more. The speck became a tiny corner of paper. She pinched it and pulled. It was a piece of Mama's writing paper.

"Rose, please," Mama said without looking up. "I asked you not to do that."

Rose pushed it back in and finished sorting.

She gathered the spoiled grapes in a towel and took them to the mares and colts. They saw her coming and jostled her greedily with their noses. Rose carefully counted out the same number of grapes for each. They nibbled her hands with their soft lips, giving her goose-flesh and making her giggle. But Rose was not in a playful mood. She was thinking hard about something else.

When the horses had eaten all the grapes, she climbed into the wagon. In the corner, next to one of the trunks, was the wooden box with the willowware dishes in it. That was also where Mama kept her writing case. She wedged it tightly into the same box, to keep the dishes from moving about on the bumpy roads.

Rose looked into the dark corner, into the box. The wrapped dishes were stacked up-right. She stuck her hand down and felt between them, one by one. It was hard to see in there. She fished with her hand around the sides of the plates and the newspaper wrapping. She felt the rough boards of the wooden box and the smooth coolness of the china. Then her hand brushed something else, something like the newspaper but different. Her fingers gripped it, and she pulled it out of the box. It was a piece of paper, but it had green printing on it. A number had been printed boldly in all four corners: "100."

Rose opened her mouth to shout. But she could not find her breath, and she wasn't sure what to shout. She climbed trembling out of the wagon and ran to the table. Mama was still writing with her head bowed.

"Mama," she managed to croak.

Mama looked up. "What is it, Rose? Why are you shaking like that?"

Rose still couldn't speak. So she laid the piece of paper down on the table, in front of Mama. Mama's eyes popped wide open. Her jaw dropped.

Rose finally blurted out, "I found it! In the wagon. In the plates!"

"But . . . but . . . how?" Mama stammered in disbelief.

"There," Rose said, pointing to the seam in

the writing case. "It fell through the crack, when it was in the wagon."

"But . . . how in Heaven's name did you know?"

Rose showed Mama the bit of white paper stuck there. Then Mama's whole face lit up. Her arms scooped Rose into a great, tight hug.

"Praise be!" Mama cried. "My wonderful, smart little girl. Now, let's find Papa. With so much hard work ahead, there isn't a moment to waste."

Going Home

Rose sat on the wagon seat between Mama and Papa. Fido sat on Mama's lap, panting contentedly. They were going home.

The ground was raw and muddy where the horses had been tethered. It was bare and dusty where the wagons had sat. Where there had been so much life all those days, there were only worn spots with rocks sticking up. That exciting summer of traveling and playing with Paul and George was truly over.

"Is it far?" asked Rose.

"Just on the other side of town," Mama said.

Rose grinned happily. They weren't going far away at all. She had been smiling ever since she found the hundred-dollar bill. When Mama had told Papa about it, a joyful look had filled his face. There had never been a more wonderful moment.

"You saved the day, Rose," Papa had said. "A father couldn't be more proud."

Now they drove through the town square. The afternoon sun lit the front of the hotel where Paul and George were living. Men sat in chairs along the high wooden sidewalk, whittling sticks of wood with knives and talking.

They passed Hoover's Livery Stable, where some boys were pitching horseshoes in the shade. Then a blacksmith shop. In no time they left behind the last houses of town and drove up a long hill. The railroad tracks ran alongside their right. On the left spread a large orchard. Rose could see spots of red that were ripening apples.

"Are we there?" Rose asked. "Is this our farm?"

"I wish it were," said Papa. "Our trees are

too little to make apples yet. But in a few years, they'll look just like those."

At the top of the road was a tall, square building with a beautiful curved roof. Big windows looked out all around. A bell tower stood above the double front doors. The ground around it was trodden bare. Beyond it was woods.

"That's the schoolhouse," Mama said. "Isn't it lovely?"

The school was shuttered and Rose thought it looked lonesome. The hitching posts were empty. No children played outside. It was harvesttime, and everyone was helping bring in the crops.

"Will Paul and George go there?" Rose asked hopefully.

"Of course," said Mama. "It's the only school in town."

Rose let out a little sigh of relief.

Over her head, Mama and Papa chatted in lively voices.

"We don't have much to fall back on, after buying salt pork and cornmeal," said Mama.

"It makes me uneasy."

"We can live off the timber for now," Papa said. "There's plenty of it. And so long as we get some land cleared, we'll have crops next summer, and grazing land for a cow or two. When the apple trees come into bearing, we'll do just fine."

"We ought to be able to pay off the mortgage by then," Mama said. "How long will it take the trees to bear?"

"I'd say five years, six for certain."

Rose was shocked. She'd be thirteen by the time she could eat their own apples!

"So long?" Mama said. "Well, I suppose we can make it till then. If we can just keep our health. I hope we haven't been too hasty, Manly."

"We went over all that, Bess," said Papa. "Just put your mind off it. Things are going to work out square, you'll see."

The road entered the woods, and the railroad veered away to the south. The wheel tracks sloped gently down, through a leafy tunnel of tree limbs. Stumps stuck up in the middle of the trail. The metal rims of the wheels rang out as the wagon jolted and lurched over rocks.

Then the road seemed to go almost straight up a long, long hill. But Papa turned Pet and May away from it, onto a faint set of tracks in a little valley.

A sparkling stream rippled alongside. It tumbled over flat ledges and flowed smoothly through shallow pools under the trees. The wagon tracks ended at one of those pools. The horses stopped to take a drink.

"Here we are!" Mama sang out. "What do you think?"

Rose looked up at the green hills surrounding the little valley. The late-afternoon sun made quivering patches of light on the water. But she didn't see a farm, or anything that looked like apple trees.

Papa tightened the reins and whistled to the mares. They raised their dripping muzzles and leaned forward to pull the wagon across the stream and up the hill.

The woods rose up in front of them. Shafts

of yellow sunlight pierced the treetops. Big flat rocks lay loose on the ground. The horses' hooves slipped and clattered on them as they struggled up the hill.

Finally Papa *whoa*ed the horses and set the brake. The wagon came to a halt in a clearing. Several gray birds with striped wings flew across it, scolding loudly. A little log house sat to one side, huddled beneath some tall trees. Dead branches and last year's leaves cluttered its roof. Piles of brush and half-cut logs lay scattered on the ground.

The house had a tumbledown look, but to Rose's eyes it was the most beautiful log house in the world. She scrambled across Mama's lap, climbed down the wagon wheel, and ran right to it.

"Be careful!" Mama called out as Rose turned the corner of the house. A rough thick door hung open from a yawning doorway. She peered inside. There was a narrow little room, a lean-to, with a hole in the roof for a cookstove chimney pipe. Dead leaves covered the packed earthen floor.

Right inside there was another open door.

Beyond it Rose found a larger room, with a wooden floor. It was dark, except for a tiny bit of daylight from the open doors behind her. The house had no windows.

The room was bare, and it smelled musty, like the woods. Dead leaves had blown into the corners. Rose stepped inside. The floor gave a startling squeak under her foot.

A big fireplace made of rocks rose up one wall. All the walls were made of logs piled on top of one another. In between the logs was dried mud that had crumbled away in places. Above her head were rafters and the underside of the wood-shingled roof.

"Rose!" Mama's muffled voice came through the walls. "Come and help unload. It'll be dark soon."

"Coming," Rose called out. Her voice sounded hollow in the empty house.

Outside, she found Fido sniffing around a pile of brush with his nose to the ground. His ears and tail stood at attention. Rose picked up one of the chairs to carry it toward the house.

"Wait," Mama said. "We're going to spend one more night in the wagon."

"Can't we sleep in the little house, Mama? Please?"

"Not until we scrub it, top to bottom," Mama said. "I never thought I'd look forward to scrubbing floors. But I can hardly wait to set up housekeeping again."

The sun set, the light faded, and the forest turned a ghostly gray. The wind died, and the trees seemed to be listening as the shadows stole in.

In the silence Rose could hear the sound of water bubbling. It chuckled from a shadowy place in a gully behind the house. Rose wanted to look, but she decided to wait until daylight.

Papa took the lantern out of the wagon. He pressed the squeaky spring to lift the globe, struck a match, and touched it to the wick. The lantern shone like a star, plunging the shadowy forest into blackness. Papa held it up, looking for a good place to hang it.

Suddenly Fido burst out barking. Rose nearly jumped out of her skin. At the edge of the lantern's circle of light stood a man! He had appeared from nowhere.

Rose scooted behind Mama. Fido stood at attention, a low growl rolling in his throat.

For the longest moment no one spoke or moved. Only the trees and bushes stirred in the wavering lamplight. The man just stood there, bony hands at his side, feet bare, big eyes gleaming at them. Patches covered his overalls. He was thin, with hollow cheeks and a long beard.

The man took a step closer. Fido gave a sharp warning bark that echoed from the gully. The man flinched. So did Rose. Mama's hand slid into the pocket of her dress, where she kept her revolver.

"Hello, there," Papa finally said.

"Hello, friend," the man answered politely. "I hate to be a bother, but I was passing by and seen your lantern light. That's why I come up these wagon tracks. Thought you might know of some work I could trade out . . . for vittles. I'm a right hard worker, and I don't drink none."

Mama's hand withdrew from her pocket.

"These are hard times," Papa said. "We know it ourselves. But as you see, we're just moving in. Took our last cent to get this place. What food I could trade would just about starve a rabbit. You ought to try in town. It's over the hill that way, 'bout a mile and a half."

The man looked around the clearing but didn't stir to leave. "You got a good place here," he said.

Papa took off his hat to scratch his head. "I guess it will be, someday," he said. "With a bit of Providence."

The man stroked his beard thoughtfully for a moment. "And a lot of work," he said. "Friend, I got to tell you the truth. I been walking these hills all day. I'm a tie hacker by trade. Know all about logging and turning trees into wooden things. But I'll do anything.

"You see, I got my wife and young'uns camped in the next hollow, over that ridge. This'll be the third day we ain't had a proper meal. Times is awful hard. And I cain't ask my horses to go another step. I just . . ." He seemed to run out of words.

"Let me think a minute," Papa said, twisting his mustache. "I reckon two men can cut twice as much wood as one. Don't know if we can sell that wood right off. But it's a small risk.

"Tell you what. Come by at daybreak. You help me cut a load to sell, and I guess I can spare some grub tonight."

Papa reached into the wagon. He pulled out the cloth sack holding the slab of salt pork.

"Manly!" Mama cried out. "We have Rose to think of."

"We don't have much," Papa said to the man. "As you can see, I have a wife and daughter myself. But I could use an experienced man about the place."

"I . . . I'm sorry," Mama said, blushing crimson. "I only meant . . ."

The man nodded.

Papa pulled his knife from its leather sheath and cut through the white meat. Then he slit the corner of the cornmeal sack and poured some into one of Mama's tin pails.

"Do you have a good ax?" Papa asked the

217

man. "Bring it if you do. We'll start at dawn and put in a good day's work. If the wood sells, I'll treat you right."

Papa handed the man the pork and the pail of cornmeal. The man began to speak, but Papa held up his hand. "Don't mention it," he said. "See you at dawn."

In a wink, the shadows had swallowed the visitor up.

Mama looked at Papa and shrugged helplessly. "I don't know what came over me," she said. "Pa would have done the same thing. He would no sooner turn a hungry stranger from his door than his own flesh and blood."

"You're right, Bess," said Papa. "We do have Rose to think of. But we'll get by. Maybe even better for having helped him."

Cleaning House

Time to get up." Mama gently shook Rose in the starry darkness before dawn. "We've a long day ahead."

Rose gathered wood for their last camp breakfast. Fido was circling the brush pile again, nose to the ground.

"What is it, Fido?" Rose asked. He looked at her, panting, and then at the brush pile. Rose peered into the dark tangle of tree limbs. It was too thick to see anything. She poked a stick in there, but nothing moved.

One by one the stars faded as the first blush of dawn appeared in the sky. Fresh breezes stirred the leaves and set the branches swaying. Waking birds chirped noisily. Two squirrels chased each other across the roof of the house.

Fido ran to the edge of the clearing and barked once. Then he came back and sat by the wagon. A moment later the stranger appeared, walking up the hill.

"He's a smart dog," said Mama. "Already he can tell between friends and strangers."

The man carried Mama's pail in his hand. On his shoulder he balanced a long metal saw. It had large wicked-looking teeth, and a wooden handle at either end.

"Morning, ma'am," he called out. He handed Mama the pail. She nearly dropped it, it was so heavy. "The missus picked 'em yesterday," he said. "She found a patch near camp. They ain't real ripe, but you got to get to 'em early, before they get bird pecked and buggy."

Mama reached into the pail and plucked out a small brown object. Rose picked one out to look at, too. Its soft skin was furry to the touch. It was shaped like a small potato, but the skin made Rose think of a mouse or a mole.

"We saw these on the trees driving here," said Mama.

"They're pawpaws," the man said. "They grow wild, where it stays good and wet. Makes a fine pudding, but they eat pretty good just plain."

"Thank you," Mama said. "I'm sure we will enjoy these."

Then Papa took his ax and went with the man to mark the trees they would cut that day.

Mama sent Rose to fetch a pail of water. "The spring is over there," she said. "In the gully next to the house."

Rose followed a worn path from the door of the log house to the edge of the gully. The path dropped down into the gully, steeper than stairs. An enormous rock stood at one end, the hollow sound of gurgling water coming from behind it. The water ran from under that rock into a little pool, as round as a wash-tub and half as deep. Then it spilled out of the pool into a little branch that wandered down-hill, between the trees.

Rose skidded down the steep path, holding on to roots and branches. The earth was smooth and cool under her feet. The sweet-smelling air was cool, too, and damp. It poured over her warm skin, waking her up all over.

She dipped her hand in the cold pool. Water spiders dimpled the surface. Black bugs on the bottom skittered away when she moved her hand. Ferns leaned over from the hillside. A hollowed-out gourd hung from a branch by a rope. Rose pulled it down and dipped herself a gourdful. The water tasted delicious. It even made her feel refreshed inside.

The spring was a peaceful, quiet place. The only sounds were the water murmuring to it-self and birds singing in the trees. Up the hill-side, above her, the woods loomed, dark and mysterious. The tips of the highest trees caught the first yellow rays of the sun.

Then something rustled in the leaves. Rose held her breath, listening. The leaves rustled again, louder. She looked for Fido, but he was nowhere to be seen.

Rose quickly filled the water pail and scrambled back up the path, as fast as she could. She decided that next time, she would take Fido.

At breakfast Papa said the stranger had showed him how to pick the best trees for cook wood. The man's name was Cyrus.

"He knows timber," Papa said. "He worked in logging camps farther east, cutting railroad ties. But then the Panic shut the camps down."

"He seems pleasant enough," Mama said. "He brought back my tin pail, and some wild fruit besides."

"I've been thinking, Bess. He could be a big help to us, so long as we can sell enough wood to support both families. If he'll just stay to help build a barn to stable the horses, we should be snug for winter."

"And a henhouse," Mama added.

"That, too," Papa said. "It sure is good to have our own place again, to be building something up for the future. And I like these woods, Bess. I feel more at home here in one day than in all those years on the prairie."

Finally, Mama and Papa finished talking and Rose could ask, "What's a Panic?"

"Well, that's what happens when folks run out of money," said Papa.

"Couldn't they make some more?" Rose asked.

Both Mama and Papa chuckled. "Some politicians in Washington think so," said Papa. "But no, Rose. You cannot make more money like more flapjacks. It must be earned. And it must be worth something. A piece of paper isn't really money until there's gold in the U.S. treasury to back it up."

Rose was going to ask another question, but Papa stood up and said, "I won't earn anything sitting here. I've got to get to work."

After breakfast Mama and Rose inspected the house. The lean-to kitchen was small, but Mama said it was better than camp cooking. Inside the house, sunlight peeked through cracks in the walls, casting ribbons of light on the floorboards. They heard a shot from Papa's gun.

"Maybe Papa shot us supper," said Mama. She walked all the way around the room, looking and thinking.

"We'll have to get Papa to chink those logs. And put in a window. This is the darkest, draftiest place I ever saw."

They set right to work. Mama carried out the old ashes from the fireplace. Rose found a piece of bark to use for a scoop, and she helped.

They knocked down all the spiderwebs with the broom and a stick. Homeless spiders scurried over the floor and walls. Rose's arms and legs crawled with imaginary spiders. She kept rubbing her skin to get rid of that feeling.

Then they swept everything out the door and out of the lean-tos: dust, balls of spider thread, mouse nests, and dead leaves. Next, Mama went down to the creek and filled a pail with clean sand. She sprinkled it on the wood floor, along with some water. Together Mama and Rose got down on their hands and knees and scrubbed that floor with wet rags, as hard as they could.

It was the most tiring chore Rose had ever

done. Her arm ached. Her back hurt. Her knuckles burned from scraping them on the floorboards. Her knees were sore from grinding into the grit. Sand got between her toes and under her fingernails. It even got on her face.

But finally the sand had scrubbed all the dark, dirty wood. They rinsed it with countless buckets of fresh water. They doused the floor until every last bit of sand and dirt had been swept into the cracks to drain away in the soil beneath.

On every trip to the spring, they paused to drink another gourdful of that delicious water. It seemed their thirst would never be quenched. Rose's stomach sloshed and gurgled when she moved.

They rested while the floor dried. The smell of wet wood mixed with the sweet green scent of the warming day. They sat on a log and watched Papa and Cyrus cut a tall dead tree with Cyrus' big two-handed saw. Papa pulled one end and Cyrus pushed. Then Cyrus pulled and Papa pushed.

They had cut almost all the way through when the tree uttered a groan and began to lean. Then it swooped to the ground with terrifying speed, crashing in a cloud of flying leaves, trembling branches, and dust.

"May I go look?" asked Rose.

"No," Mama said. "Felling trees is very dangerous work, Rose. You must not play in the woodlot. We'll look later, when they aren't cutting.

"Now, how shall we arrange the furniture?" she asked. She drew a square in the dirt. "That is the house," she said. "And this is the chimney." She drew a little square on one side of the big square.

"Where shall we put the big bed?" Mama asked.

Rose looked at the square for a minute. "By the fireplace? To stay warm in winter."

"That's a good idea," Mama said. She drew a little rectangle next to the fireplace and away from the door. Rose was looking at the picture in the dirt when Mama suddenly burst out, "Oh, my . . . land!"

Mama jumped off the log. She grabbed her skirt in both hands and shook it hard. She looked around her frantically, as if something might fall out.

"My land!" she shouted again. "Rose, come away from that log!"

Rose was so astonished she couldn't move. She looked where Mama had been sitting. At first her eyes did not believe what they saw. Staring back at her was the biggest spider she had ever seen. It was as big as a person's hand! Its huge body and long thick legs were covered in black and reddish-brown fur, as sleek as horsehair.

It reached out with its front legs and began crawling right toward Rose!

Rose leaped up. Her breath came in gasps. She picked up a stick and stood there, ready to hit it but afraid to try. That spider was so big it might chase her!

"I . . . I've never seen anything so gruesome," Mama said. They watched as the spider waved and reached out with its giant legs. It was terrifyingly beautiful.

Papa came running, rifle in his hand. Cyrus carried the ax. "I heard you shout, Bess! What is it? Did you find a snake?"

"Just look at it," Mama said, pointing.

They all looked. But the log was bare. The spider had slipped away in an instant.

"It was a spider," Mama said. "As big as . . . as *this*." She held up her hand and spread her fingers. "Covered with hair!"

Papa twisted his mustache in silence. He gently stirred the leaves with the rifle barrel.

"Be careful, Manly," Mama said. "It might be angry."

Cyrus leaned on the ax and chuckled. Mama glared at him.

"Sorry, ma'am," he said. "I didn't mean no offense. It's just . . . well, I guess them critters'd give anybody a good fright that never seen one."

"What is it?" asked Rose. She wanted to look at the spider again, to see its fur. But there was no sign of it anywhere.

"It's a tarantula," he said. "You'd never have cause to shoot it. I never did hear of one biting nobody, and they ain't poisonous even if it did. You see 'em mostly round this time of year. They're looking for dens for the winter, I guess."

Papa mopped his forehead.

Mama took a deep breath. "You don't suppose it was living in the house, do you?" she said.

"Could be," said Cyrus. "Maybe you bothered it. But don't you worry, ma'am. Boys take tarantulas to school right in their pants pockets, to scare the little girls with. They cain't be too harmful at that."

"I have never had such a fright," said Mama, laughing at herself. "I heard your gun, Manly. Did you get a rabbit?"

"Rattlesnake," said Papa. "We killed one this morning."

"Rattlesnakes, huge hairy spiders," said Mama. "What else will we find in these woods?"

Moving In

Rose was jumpy all during dinner and after, when she helped Mama unpack the wagon. She looked before she sat down. She kicked at piles of leaves. Little noises startled her.

Mama was thinking about the spider, too. She scratched her ankles as if something were crawling on them. She looked into boxes before she reached with her hand.

"My imagination is playing tricks on me," she said.

Seeing Mama scratch made Rose itch too.

First they unpacked Mama and Papa's

231

bedstead and bedspring. There was trail dust on the undersides, which they brushed off. Then they took out Rose's trundle bed, which fit perfectly underneath. They put the beds in the corner, near the fireplace, right where Rose had suggested. They put the table on the other side of the fireplace, near the door.

They cleaned out the little camp stove and put it in the lean-to. Mama would never have to cook outdoors again.

The trunks were too heavy to lift without Papa's help, so they opened them in the wagon and carried in the linen and clothing, a little at a time. Mama put the hanging clothes on a rope tied between two rafters.

Then Rose helped make up the beds. Mama shook open the crisp sheets with a sharp *snap!* The musty smell of the trunk was in those sheets. For a moment Rose thought of De Smet.

First they made the big bed together. Then Rose made up her trundle bed by herself. She tucked the corners of the sheets in snugly, the way Mama made the big bed. Then she laid her quilt on top and smoothed it out. Rose was delighted to see it tidy, all ready to crawl into. They really were going to sleep inside that night!

They each carried in a stack of the willowware china. Rose was happy to see those plates again. She was tired of the flimsy tin plates they used for camping. She had missed the beautiful scene that always waited under her food. It was a picture, painted in the most beautiful blue, of a faraway land where feathery trees grew next to fanciful houses. Some people hurried over a bridge to play with their friends. A garden path led to—

"Rose!" Mama called. Rose stopped short and looked up. She was just two steps away from a tree. A moment more and she would have smacked right into it!

"What are you staring at so hard?" asked Mama.

"I was looking at the picture on the plate."

"Let's not tempt fate, Rose," said Mama. "It's already a miracle nothing broke at the Missouri River."

Mama carried in the glass bread platter. She and Papa had given it to each other their first Christmas. She propped it carefully on the fireplace mantel, where they could look at it. The dim light from the doorway glinted along the edges. Raised letters said "GIVE US THIS DAY" across the top and "OUR DAILY BREAD" across the bottom. Hundreds of loaves of Mama's delicious bread had been served on that platter. Just looking at it made Rose hungry.

In the bottom of one trunk, Mama found the rag rug Aunt Carrie had braided for a going-away present. She spread it in front of the fireplace. It gave the little house a cheerful look.

Next she brought in the wooden clock with the carved wooden leaf on the top. A glass door with gilded vines and leaves on it protected the face. Gilded birds perched in the vines.

Mama set the clock on the mantel, beside the bread plate. She wound it with the key and set the time by the nickel-plated alarm clock.

Then she gave the pendulum a little push, to start it swinging.

"Now, let's put out the green gingham tablecloth, and we're finished," Mama said. After the cloth was all smoothed out, she stood back in the doorway with her hands on her hips and looked at the room.

Just then the clock chimed five times. Every corner of the house filled with the clear, round tones. When the last echo faded away, the little house was brimming with life.

"Time to think about supper," Mama said. "Papa has been cutting wood all day. He'll be hungry. Run and ask him how much longer he'll be."

Rose found Papa and Cyrus still cutting, next to a big pile of chopped and split logs.

"Hello, Rose," Papa said. "How goes the moving in?"

"It's done," Rose said happily. "It's a real house now. Mama wants to know when to make supper."

"You tell her we'll quit when the light's gone."

So they kept cutting, even after the sun went down. When it was dark, Cyrus went back over the ridge to his wagon. Mama held the lantern while Papa took the canopy and side curtains off the wagon.

"Doesn't look like much, does it?" Papa said wearily. "It's hard to believe we traveled all that way in it."

Papa drove the wagon to the pile of wood. He set the lamp on the wagon seat, and Mama and Rose helped him stack the stove wood in the wagon-box. Rose brought wood to Mama, who handed the split logs up to Papa, two at a time. He stacked the logs in rows and in layers, higher and higher, until the hack could hold no more without its falling out.

"I'm all done in," Papa said. They were all exhausted. And hungry. One at a time they washed their hands and faces in the basin that Mama had set on a chair just outside the door. Then they dried themselves on the towel that was hung over the chair back.

Papa walked into the lean-to kitchen and started to open the inside door into the house, but Mama stopped him. "Shoes off, if you please. No need to spoil our hard work on the floor."

Papa pulled off his shoes and sighed with relief, "Ahhh," he said, rubbing his ankles.

"Wait, just one minute," Mama said, and disappeared behind the door into the house. Rose heard the clink of the lamp chimney being lifted, and the sound of a match striking. She quickly wiped her bare feet on the edge of the sill. Then she scurried through the door into the house. She wanted to see Papa's face when he came in. Mama had said Fido must stay outside.

"You may come in now," Mama called to Papa.

Papa opened the door slowly. His tired eyes shone happily in the dim light. "Well, I'll be . . ." he said. He slowly looked around the room. Then Rose looked too. So did Mama. Even though they had worked on it all day, this was the first time they had really seen it as their new home.

The lamp flame purred quietly on the table,

throwing its soft yellow circle of light on the settings. Mama had turned the wick up so Papa could see better.

The bread platter sat in the middle of the table with three big pieces of crusty corn bread on it. The air was rich with the creamy smell of beans bubbling on the stove.

The little sewing chest that Papa had made for Mama out of old cigar boxes stood near the bed. Its polished wood gleamed in the lamplight. The autograph quilt that the family and friends in De Smet had sewed for them lay neatly on the big bed. Papa's good hat hung from a peg by the front door. He went over and picked it up.

"A fellow knows he's home when he has his own place to hang his hat," said Papa. Mama looked at him with soft eyes. Her face glowed with pride. The clock filled the silence with its peaceful ticking.

"I don't know how you girls did it," Papa finally said. "But anybody would swear we've lived here our whole lives." He gave Mama a great hug and a long kiss that made her gasp when he finally let go.

Then Papa picked Rose up by the waist and held her high over his head. "You are a mite big for this, Rose. I remember when you were so little, you had to stand twice in a place to make a shadow."

He gave her a big, bristly kiss and hugged her hard.

"And now," he said. "I'm sure we could all do with some supper. I'm as hungry as a spring bear."

Sleepless Night

All through supper they chattered like a flock of sparrows.

Papa told Mama and Rose about the things Cyrus had said about Missouri. "The woods are full of small game," Papa said. "There's cash money to be made trapping. He showed me raccoon tracks, and he says there are usually plenty of rabbits and squirrels. There are deer and wild turkeys, too. Who would have guessed settled country could be so bountiful?"

"Are there wolves?" Rose asked. She wanted to see a wolf up close, the way Mama had as a little girl.

"Yes. Cyrus says there are a few wolves," Papa said. "And even panthers."

Panthers scared Rose. She did not ever want to meet one.

"What's a raccoon, Papa?"

"It's a small animal that has gray fur and black patches around its eyes. It sleeps in the daytime and hunts its food at night.

"I'm sorry to be scratching at the table, Bess," Papa said suddenly. "Something is biting the dickens out of me, top and bottom!"

Without thinking about it, Mama and Rose scratched at their legs. Then, all at once, they looked at each other and realized they were all scratching.

"Some pest is biting us," Mama said, hitching up her dress. There were three red welts on her ankles. She rubbed them and winced.

"Whatever it is, they itch like nothing I've ever met with," Papa said. "Even the mosquitoes in Big Slough weren't this bad."

Rose looked at her legs. She hadn't noticed, but now she saw that she had red blotches, too.

They all scratched. But it didn't help. Instead, the bites burned and throbbed and itched even more.

Papa yawned a great yawn. "Excuse my manners. I'm all done in, itches or not. And there's a big day ahead tomorrow."

They all went to bed. It was cozy to climb under the covers in their new house. Rose was tired, but she lay awake for a long time, thinking about raccoons and panthers and big furry spiders. She listened to the insects singing in the trees and scratched her legs. But the itch just went deeper, where she couldn't reach it. She twisted and turned and sighed. She rubbed her burning ankles on the cool sheets. But in a second they were hot and itchy again.

She heard Mama and Papa twisting and turning and scratching and sighing, too.

Then, after what seemed like the longest time of twisting and turning, Rose heard a scrabbling sound nearby. She lay perfectly still, listening. A tingle of fear raced up her back. Her legs begged to be scratched, but she forced herself to lie still and listen.

She heard a scampering sound. Then more scrabbling right near her bed. Rose turned her head, but it was too dark to see anything. She could barely breathe. Her eyes ached from straining to see into the darkness.

From his sleeping place outside the front door, Fido barked. A second later, Rose felt something like fingers scampering across her legs.

She kicked her legs as hard as she could.

"MAMA! PAPA!" she shrieked. "Something's in here!"

Now there were tiny scampering sounds everywhere in the house. Mama got up quickly to light the lamp. When the match burst into flame, Rose saw two tiny dots of light in the corner. They winked and vanished.

"Manly!" Mama said, rubbing the back of her left leg with her right foot. "There are rats in here! They've chewed the corner off the sack of cornmeal."

Fido whined outside the door.

Rose tiptoed across the floor and sat on the

big bed. She did not want her feet touching the floor where the rats had been.

Now they were all up, itchy and sleepy, wondering what to do. Rose didn't feel very cozy in the house now.

"Rose can't sleep on the floor with rats running across her," said Mama. "She should sleep with us in the big bed."

"Yes, I suppose," Papa said in a croaky voice. He was too tired to be upset. He sat at the table, his head resting on his hand. His eyes were closed.

Fido barked sharply at the door. Then he scratched at it. Mama took the lamp and went to see.

"He's caught a rat!" Mama said when she came back. "He brought it to the door, the little show-off. You don't suppose . . . Manly? Are you awake?"

"I'm listening, Bess," Papa said with closed eyes.

"Perhaps we could let Fido in for a spell."

"Could we?" Rose cried.

"Just until the rats are gone," Mama said.

"We could let him stay indoors for tonight. To see how he does."

Papa opened an eye. "Sounds better than doing nothing," he said. "Let's see what Fido's made of."

Rose ran into the lean-to and opened the front door. Fido sat there, panting excitedly.

"Come in, Fido," Rose said. He pranced in, leaving his catch behind. For all the noise those rats had made, Rose didn't think they were very big to look at. But they were ugly just the same.

Fido gave Rose's foot a grateful lick and ran over to lick Papa's hand. Then, as they all watched him, he ran about, sniffing along the walls.

He stopped at one of the corners. He twisted his head this way and that. Finally he sat down and stared at one place in the floor-boards. Rose saw a hole that she had not noticed before.

Mama put out the lamp and they all went back to bed; Rose lay between Mama and Papa. But they hardly slept. They could hear

Fido's nails clicking about the room. He whined some, and he growled some. Then they heard growling and scurrying and squeaking sounds that they knew must be Fido catching a rat.

Finally, it was quiet. Rose had just begun to fall asleep when she felt a soft hand on her forehead. "Time to get up, Rose," said Mama's tired voice.

Mama lit the lamp low, and Papa and Rose got out of bed. Fido was sleeping by the door. Here and there were little bits of dark fur. Fido raised his head and blinked sleepily.

"Well, there's one thing certain, and two things sure," Papa said. "That little fella can earn his keep."

The Orchard

Mama baked extra corn bread for breakfast and fried up an extra bit of salt pork. She packed them in a tin pail for Papa's dinner. Then she and Rose watched him drive the loaded wagon down the hill to town. Little Pet whinnied to her mother from the shady spot where Papa had tied the colts so they wouldn't follow.

"Good luck!" Mama called after the rumbling wagon.

"Don't wait supper!" Papa called back, waving his hat. "I won't be home until the whole load is sold!"

When the wagon's rumble died away, they knew Papa had driven over the far hill, into Mansfield. The thuds of Cyrus' ax rang in the wood lot. Rose said a little prayer to herself, that Papa would sell the whole wagonload.

They washed the dishes, made the beds, and swept out the house. Then Mama said, "Let's go soak our legs in the spring. Perhaps it will take some of the itch out of these bites."

They sat on rocks at the edge of the pool. Warm sunshine speckled the ground and played in wavy lines on the pool's bottom. Rose's skin felt parched and thirsty for that cold, clear water. Her legs tingled as she slowly lowered them in. Her skin broke out in deliciously shivery goose bumps.

Mama took off her shoes and sighed as she dipped her toes in the water. "This is much better."

"Where are the apple trees, Mama?" Rose asked.

"Just over the hill. We'll walk there later."

After their legs were refreshed, they

climbed the steep hill above the spring. It was rocky and thick with trees. A bird like a prairie hen ran off through the dead leaves. Mama said it was probably a kind of quail.

"I'm sorry I left my shoes by the pool," Mama said, stepping carefully over a rocky spot. "These sharp stones hurt my feet."

Rose's feet were tough from going barefoot all summer. She didn't even notice those rocks, except where they were warm from the sun.

At the top of the hill they were nearly high enough to see across the wooded valley into Mansfield. They could just see the bell tower on the school, poking up above the trees. Great turkey vultures soared in wide graceful circles high above the valley.

Rose and Mama walked down the other side of the hill, into a big clearing. Rows of little trees lay on their sides. There were hundreds of them, more than Rose could count. Their roots had been tucked into slashes in the soil, like feet under a blanket.

Those were the apple trees, Mama said, waiting to be planted in the orchard. The trees were short and spindly. Not one of them was even as big as a single branch of the trees they had seen along the way.

They walked a little farther, to a field where some apple trees had been properly planted. They were very far apart, sticking up from small dirt mounds. In between, jagged stumps poked out of the ground. Brush piles lay around the field's edge. Their orchard didn't look anything like the beautiful, tidy orchards they had passed.

"The trees are so small," said Rose. "Will they ever get big enough to make apples?"

"Before you know it, the branches of those little trees will grow until one day they can touch one another," said Mama. "And then folks in Kansas City and Memphis will be baking our apples into pies."

Looking at those tiny, fragile trees, Rose could not believe it. She remembered she would be thirteen years old before the trees bore fruit. That time seemed even further off, now.

Mama and Rose walked around the rest of the farm. It was all woods. Papa would have to cut many trees that winter to get the apple saplings all planted by spring.

The ground was rocky almost everywhere. In some places huge boulders stuck out of the ground. But Mama said Papa would clear the land and someday they would have smooth, rolling meadows and pastureland.

"For now, it is a very rocky ridge of land," said Mama. She looked at Rose, her face suddenly bright. "There's a thought. We can call the place Rocky Ridge Farm. What do you think?"

Rose liked the sound of it. It was easy to say, and it was true.

"I like it," she said.

"That's it, then," Mama said with satisfaction. "We'll tell Papa tonight. Someday, Rose, folks will come to visit us, and they'll see acres of beautiful orchard trees, cows in the pasture, sheep in the meadow, and corn in the field. They'll ask, Why is it called Rocky Ridge Farm? And we can tell them. That way we will never forget how it was when we first saw it."

A New Friend

After dinner, Mama said Rose could explore on her own, but she must take Fido with her.

They went to the spring, where Rose drank a cool gourdful of water while Fido lapped a drink for himself. Then she decided to follow the spring branch, to see where it went. The water trickled downhill through a tunnel of shade. Briars snatched at her dress. Low limbs of trees stretched across her way.

She heard a rustling sound. Fido had disappeared in the bushes, so Rose picked up a long stick. She beat the leaves and bushes in front of her as she walked, to scare away any snakes or tarantula spiders that might be lurking about.

At the bottom of the hill, the trickling water ran into the creek. Rose turned left and walked along the bank. She could barely hear the ringing of Cyrus' ax.

Right next to the creek, she found a tree with small round fruits the size of plums hanging from its branches. The air there smelled ripe and summery. The hanging fruits were orange and yellow. But some that had smashed on the ground were dark brown. A perfume like spilled molasses rose from them. Honeybees buzzed around the oozy lumps.

Rose had never seen that fruit before. She knew she shouldn't try to eat one without asking Mama, or offering it to the horses. But if bees like it, she thought, I will too. She touched her finger to one of the fallen fruits, where the skin had cracked. She tasted it. It was sweet, although not as sweet as a plum.

She hit the trunk with the palm of her hand. Some of the fruit fell with a pattering noise on the flinty rocks, then rolled off into the leaves. Rose picked one up. It was a beautiful warm yellow-orange, with a little blush of purple. The smooth skin felt cool in her hand. She just knew it would taste sweet and juicy, so she took a bite.

At first the taste was nothing—not sweet, but not tart, either. It was just a bit crunchy. Then she felt a strange roughness in her mouth. The inside of her mouth began to shrivel. It turned dry, first cottony dry, and then as dry as dust. The insides of her lips stuck to her teeth. Her tongue stuck to her palate and a puckery feeling filled her whole mouth. It was the worst thing Rose had ever tasted, and it scared her. That fruit was poisoning her.

"Ungh! Ungh!" she coughed. Tears welled up in her eyes.

Suddenly Rose heard laughter. She looked up. Standing in front of her was a freckle-faced girl about her size. She was wearing a bright-yellow calico dress. Her fiery red hair was pulled into pigtails. Her eyes were the clearest, brightest blue Rose had ever seen. She looked at Rose haughtily.

"Your face looks like my pa's tobacco pouch," the girl said mockingly. "Serves you right, I guess. Those are my pa's persimmons."

Rose tried to spit out the horrible-tasting fruit. But her mouth was too dry and puckery. So she pulled it out with her finger. After a few moments her mouth began to feel right again.

Now Rose's face blazed hot. She was embarrassed and angry.

But she tried to remember her manners. "I'm sorry," she stammered. "I didn't know it was your tree."

"Where're you from?" the little girl asked, hands on her hips. But she didn't wait for Rose to answer. "You ain't from around here, or you'd of knowed better'n to eat a green persimmon. Are you from that wagon in the hollow over yonder? My pa don't like drifters. He won't like it one bit if I tell him covered wagon folks was stealing his persimmons."

Rose was stunned. She didn't like what the little girl was saying. But she shouldn't have been taking someone else's . . . what did she call them?

Rose knew one thing for sure: "We aren't drifters, either. We live here. That's our farm. Right back there."

"Well, then," the girl said. "That's a different story, ain't it? Why didn't you say so? We're neighbors. My pa says you got to be neighborly to neighbors. So you go right on. Them persimmons mostly rot by the time we pick them. And the possums always steal a mess. We got more persimmon trees down the creek anyway. Where'd you say your farm's at?"

"Up there," Rose said. She pointed up the hill, back toward the spot where the spring branch met the creek.

"That must be Mr. White's place, with all them little apple trees he bought," the girl said.

"We just moved into our house," said Rose. "With my dog, Fido." Rose looked around, but

Fido was nowhere to be seen.

"Well, this is my pa's place, on this side of Fry Creek," the little girl said proudly. "I've lived here my whole life, eight years. I'm the baby. How old are you?"

"I'll be eight in December," said Rose. "But I'm the only one."

"I got two big sisters," the girl said. "Cora and Mary Sue don't like farm work much. They help my ma with the cookin' and house chores. They sew a bunch, too. I hate sewing."

"Yes, sewing is hard," said Rose, although she didn't hate sewing at all. She liked to see what she could make, and Mama often told stories when they sewed together. But Rose didn't want to disagree with the girl.

"What I like is helpin' my pa in the barn and out in the fields. I ain't never going to school and sit with no stuck-up town girls. Besides," she said, "my pa says I'm the best son a man could ever hope for. What's your name?"

"Rose. Rose Wilder. I came with my mama and papa from South Dakota."

"South Dakota? What's it like there?" the little girl asked.

"It's prairie," Rose explained. "It's all grass. And windy. But there's a drought now. All the crops are dying. And there aren't any trees."

"No trees!" the little girl shouted. "Where do the birds put their nests? What about squirrels? You mean you got no squirrels there?"

"No," Rose said.

"How 'bout 'coons, or 'possum?"

"No," Rose said. "But there are jackrabbits, and gophers."

The little girl just shook her head. "Gophers," she said. "Like a groundhog? That ain't no animals."

Then she told Rose about persimmons. "These ain't ripe yet," she said, showing Rose a persimmon like the one she had bitten into. It was firm, and the color was lighter than the others. "They're puckery. You cain't eat 'em till they get soft. These kind here have tandy acid in 'em. That's what my pa calls it, I think. Here's a real good ripe one. See? It's dark and kind of mushy. My ma cooks them in pudding.

Smack down on it."

Rose took a small bite. This time her mouth filled with the dark flavor of sweet juice. It was unlike anything she had tasted. She ate all of it, spitting out the slimy brown seeds.

"There ain't too many ripe ones yet," the girl said. "'Round frost time they all start turning sweet. But you got to beat the 'possums to 'em.

"Well, I got to go. Looks like rain, and I got to help Pa with the milking. If you want to have some fun, you ought to come with me of a day and see my trap line. Come winter, I get rabbits and 'coons and 'possums and skunks."

Rose did not know what a trap line was, but she thought she would like to see one. "Yes. That would be fun," she said.

"Well, see you," the girl called.

"Good-bye," Rose said. Then she remembered something. "Wait! What's your name?"

"Alva. Alva Stubbins. See you, Rose."

Waiting for Papa

Rose gathered a few ripe persimmons in her skirt and raced home. Fido met her along the way. The last bit of sunshine vanished behind the clouds as a gust of wind stirred the leaves. Lightning flickered in the sky. The coming storm growled in its throat. Rose ran faster. She must hurry if she expected to beat it.

Then the wind stopped. Not a leaf moved. The forest became very still. Rose's and Fido's running feet seemed to rustle loudly in the leaves, and the water in the creek went on foolishly chuckling.

Finally Rose burst into the clearing, still clutching the persimmons in her skirt. Mama was pulling the chicken coop inside the lean-to. The chickens squawked complaints, and stray feathers floated in the air.

"Thank goodness," Mama said. "There you are."

Just then a tongue of lightning licked overhead. Rose and Mama flinched. They stepped back inside the door with Fido as thunder crashed on the hill and rolled away in the valley. Rose trembled with excitement.

"I'm sorry, Mama," she finally managed. "I only went a little ways . . . for a walk. I wanted to see where the spring goes."

"You look as if you might have been wrestling with a bear," Mama said. "Your braids are undone and your foot's bleeding. What's in your skirt?"

Before Rose could tell Mama her story, the forest uttered a long, shuddering sigh from all its slopes. Then the rain came, a gray curtain rushing through the trees. The roof erupted into a roaring drum. The leaves trembled, and the ground teemed with dancing drops. A gust of cool, refreshing air blew in the doorway.

"Rain!" Mama shouted above the noise. "Such a lively sound."

She shut the door against the wet gusts. They could hardly hear each other speak. Bright flashes of lightning flickered between the unchinked logs. Then the logs trembled with thunder.

"Mama, look! The roof is leaking."

They rushed around placing pots under each of the leaks. Mama pulled the bed away from the wall so it wouldn't get wet. But even with the leaks, the room was cozy in the lamplight.

Rose put the four persimmons on the table. She told Mama about her walk along Fry Creek, and about the little girl, Alva. Then Mama nibbled one of the little fruits.

"These are delicious." She cut one open with a knife. The meat was soft, and divided into sections. In the middle were large brown seeds, bigger than watermelon seeds. "I'm sure I can make something with these. But they are rather pulpy for pie."

"Alva's ma makes pudding," Rose remembered.

"When they're ripe, we must get some and try," said Mama. She went to the lean-to door to see if the storm had passed. Then she got out the scrap bag that had been packed away all summer in the wagon.

"Come sit with me on the bed," Mama said. "We can start piecing a new quilt while we wait for Papa."

Mama began by spreading out the bits of cloth on the bed. Then she laid the pattern on them at various angles to see how best to cut the scraps without waste. With her sharp shears, she cut out the squares and triangles she would stitch together to make the quilt.

She held up a scrap for Rose to see. "That's the turkey-red dress your aunt Grace wore the time she recited 'Curfew Shall Not Ring Tonight,'" Mama said. "How lovely she looked.

"And this is the last bit of that dress Grandma hated so. She wore it every summer to please Grandpa, because he'd bought the goods to surprise her. But she never could bear plaids.

"And here! This is the dress I wore to the Fourth of July, that time the horses ran away. You were too little to remember that." Mama sighed. "A quilt is something human, Rose. There isn't one of my dresses I wouldn't mind having a scrap of right now."

Rose fingered her blue calico. It was her oldest, most faded dress. It was tight in the arms, and it had a big patch on the seat. But someday a piece of it would remind her of the journey to Missouri.

"Tell me a story, Mama. Please?"

"All right," said Mama. "Let me think." A locomotive whistled in the distance.

"Did I tell you Grandpa's story about the time Mr. Edwards ran a foot race against a train?"

"No!" Rose shouted excitedly. "Tell me."

Rose and Mama sewed quilt pieces together while Mama told it:

"One day Grandpa was coming home from

buying lumber in Tracy. The train he was on was loaded with a shipment of coal, and the wind was blowing so fiercely from the west that it slowed the engine.

"Mr. Edwards was on the train, too. He was a friend of Grandpa's. Mr. Edwards was a good man, but he was a gambler, and always restless. 'I could go faster on my own two feet,' Mr. Edwards said to Grandpa in a good loud voice.

"Grandpa knew Mr. Edwards pretty well. He looked at him with a twinkle in his eye and said, good and loud, 'For how long?'

"'Long enough to outrun that little whiffet of an engine,' Mr. Edwards bragged.

"Mr. Edwards was slender, and not very hearty-looking. Some of the other passengers got to thinking. They bet Mr. Edwards he couldn't do it.

"Mr. Edwards said right away he'd show them. Grandpa never gambled, of course," Mama said solemnly. "But he held the money while Mr. Edwards tried. People always trusted Grandpa.

"So Mr. Edwards jumped out of the passenger car and started to run. He had good strong legs, and the wind could hardly catch him, he was so thin. Slowly he gained, passing one freight car and then another and another. Finally, he was running beside the puffing engine.

"'Hey, mister!' Mr. Edwards called to the engineer. 'Want the boys to get out and push?' You never saw such a surprised look as that engineer had on his face. Everyone had a great laugh, and Mr. Edwards waited for the passenger car to catch up, so he could jump on and collect his bet."

Rose laughed through a big yawn. Mama's soothing voice and the steady drumming of the rain on the roof relaxed her. She laid down her sewing and stretched out on her stomach on the bed. She closed her eyes and just listened to the rain.

It seemed like only a minute later that a gust of cool air blew on her face. But Rose realized she had been fast asleep. Mama was standing in the open doorway looking out.

Papa must be home!

Rose walked sleepily to the door and looked out. But there was no wagon in the clearing. The storm was ending. The last drops of rain felt cool on her face. A roaring sound came from the gully, and the sound of it grew in her ear.

"What is it?" asked Rose.

"It's rain water, rushing down to the creek from the spring," Mama said. She was quiet a moment. Then she asked, "Do you hear a wagon?"

Rose listened. But the roaring of the branch covered up all the other sounds. "No, I can't hear anything," she said.

The hills were dark. The clouds parted in the west, showing the last pale light of sunset. Then the hole in the clouds slowly closed and there was only darkness. Mama and Rose went back into the house. Mama was quiet as she stirred corn batter.

After Rose set the table, she lay on the bed, looking through her lesson book. Mama said it was time Rose started her studies.

"You'll be going to school next year, after we're settled," Mama said. "For now I need you to help me here. But that's no excuse for not keeping up."

Rose was glad to see her McGuffey's reader again. It wasn't as exciting as *Robinson Crusoe*, but Rose liked reading everything. In De Smet she had even read the *Chicago Inter-Ocean*, a newspaper that Papa sometimes brought home. She didn't understand all the words, but it didn't matter.

Rose knew that words were a kind of magic that anybody could make. Words told stories, which Rose loved better than anything. She thought about making up her own words, even her own secret language. She could teach words of it to Fido so that when she spoke them, only he would know what she meant.

"Why don't you read me something while I'm cooking?" Mama said. Rose flipped the pages until she found a poem, "Alice's Supper."

*"Far down in the valley the wheat grows deep,
   And the reapers are making the cradles
      sweep;
   And this is the song that I hear them sing,
   While cheery and loud their voices ring:
   ''Tis the finest wheat that ever did grow!
   And it is for Alice's supper—ho! ho!'*

"Mama!" Rose shouted.

"Yes—I heard it, too, Rose."

They could plainly hear a rattling wagon coming closer. And it was coming up the hill. Mama hurriedly lit the lantern. "Take this and go help your father while I get supper on the table. He'll be hungry."

Rose ran outside. The horses' faces bobbed into the lantern light. Their bellies were wet and their legs were covered with mud. Papa reined in the horses and jumped down. Rose ran to hug him. He smelled of wet clothes.

Then she stood on the wheel to look into the wagon-box. There were only bits of bark and wet leaves stuck to the bottom.

"You sold it all!" Rose shouted.

"I told you I wouldn't come home until I did," Papa said, smiling proudly.

Mama came out the door, wiping her hands on her apron.

"I'll tell you all about it, Bess," said Papa. "Soon as I get the team unhitched. But you can stop your worrying. Everything's going to work out fine for us here."

"There's a fresh change of clothes waiting," Mama said. "And a good hot meal."

Mama fidgeted around the house until Papa finally got washed and changed and came to supper. As soon as grace was over, Mama said, "Well, Manly. What did you get for it?"

"Seventy-five cents," said Papa. "It won't put us in clover. I had to make a good price to get rid of the last of it. But we can sell what we cut this winter, enough to get by."

"Thank heavens," Mama said. "Now if Cyrus will only stay to help cut it."

The Henhouse

Papa sat in a chair, sharpening the ax with a metal file. The cold, rasping sound of it made Rose shiver. Mama mixed pancake batter for breakfast in a bowl on the table.

"I asked somebody in town about those bites," said Papa. "It's a kind of bug called chiggers."

Rose giggled. "Chiggers?" The word tickled her. She was dressing her rag doll with tiny calico scraps Papa had brought her from Reynolds.

"They're too small to see," said Papa.

"They live in the grass and bushes."

"Are they harmful?" Mama asked. "Can we get rid of them?"

"Don't think so," said Papa. "Some folks tie rags soaked in coal oil around their ankles when they do field work. And some farmers burn off the fields and brushy places, to get rid of them."

"Sounds like a waste of coal oil, if you ask me," Mama said. "And who would start a fire on purpose? What if the wind should come up?"

"Chiggers seem to be just a fact of life in these hills," Papa said. "And ticks. They talk about them both in one breath. But their season is about finished. We won't see them again till spring."

"What about the Cooleys?" Mama said. "How did you find them?"

"They have their hands full," said Papa. "Mrs. Cooley especially, in the kitchen. George helps her with the chores. Paul is already working behind the front desk, doing as good a job as any grown man. They're working hard, but they sure landed on their feet in this town. The whole family's working, right from the get-go."

The days on Rocky Ridge Farm began to have a rhythm, like notes in a melody. Papa and Cyrus cut wood from lamplight to lamplight. Some days, Papa drove a wagonload to town. Soon he had steady customers. Then he didn't have to drive around all day selling the wood. On other days, he did chores around the farm. He and Cyrus fixed the leaky roof, plugged the rat hole, and put a snug new door on the lean-to.

Each morning, Rose helped Mama water and feed the chickens their cornmeal. The hens ran free during the day. Fido kept them safe from hawks and woods creatures. He even helped Mama and Rose find the nests, and he didn't eat a single egg.

Each afternoon they collected all the eggs they could find. Then Rose went to the wood-lot to get clean sawdust. Papa helped her scoop it up into her skirt, which she held out like a sack. In the lean-to, Rose held an empty feed sack open while Mama sprinkled the sawdust into it. Mama laid in some eggs and sprinkled more sawdust on top. She kept making layers of sawdust and eggs until she was out of eggs. Then she threw the leftover sawdust on the earth floor, to keep the mud down.

When Papa went to town, he took the sack to Reynolds and traded the eggs for credit. He used that credit to buy the things they needed, such as flour, salt pork, ax handles, and harness leather. Sometimes Papa brought home a treat for Rose: a new hair ribbon or a piece of stick candy.

At sundown each day, the chickens flew into the branches of a big tree to sleep. Fido could not protect them there. One night Rose woke up to horrible screeching. Fido barked furiously.

"What is it?" Rose screamed.

Mama hurriedly lit the lantern and bolted for the door.

"Wait, Bess," Papa shouted, untangling his pant legs. "You don't know what's out there."

He snatched his rifle off the wall and hurried to catch up with Mama. The horrible screeching stopped. Rose sat in bed, wondering what could have made such an awful sound.

"An owl carried off one of the chickens," Mama said when they came back to bed. "It looks like the one with the twisted foot. She was my best layer, too. This won't do, Manly. I need a henhouse."

In the morning, Rose found white chicken feathers scattered on the ground near the tree.

That day, Cyrus helped Papa build Mama's henhouse. They built it near the gully, to be close to water, and near the log house, so they could hear the chickens squawk if a raccoon or a snake came near.

The henhouse was square, with a slanted roof to shed rain. The walls were small tree trunks laid on top of each other and notched at the ends to fit snugly. Then Papa and Cyrus sealed the cracks with clay mud from the creek. That left no spaces for snakes to sneak through, or cold air to blow in.

It had a big door on leather hinges for Mama and Rose to bring feed and water through, and so they could clean the henhouse. Then Papa built a little door in the side. A piece of flat wood fitted into a slot to close it. Mama showed Rose how to lift the door up to let the chickens out in the morning.

"That door must always be closed at night, after the chickens are in," Mama said. "Don't forget that, Rose. Otherwise, a raccoon or fox could walk right in and kill every last bird."

The last thing Papa made was a roosting ladder inside, and two wooden shelves for the chickens to nest on.

"We need lots of leaves to put on the floor," Mama said. "Chickens like to have dry feet." Rose made many trips with her skirt full of leaves until the floor was covered.

Then the henhouse was ready.

But when it came time to roost, not one chicken headed for the door. They began to stretch their necks, eyeing their old roosting tree.

"Let's try herding them," said Mama. "But

gently. If we scare them, they won't lay. You stand on one side, and I'll stand on the other. We'll walk toward the henhouse and see if they will go in."

They gently shooed the chickens toward the door. But when they got close to the henhouse, the chickens darted past Rose and Mama into the clearing. Two chickens walked near the little doorway. They cocked their heads and looked at it suspiciously. Then they scooted away.

Mama made a little trail of cornmeal on the ground, leading to the doorway. She scattered a handful inside. The chickens greedily pecked up all the cornmeal on the ground. When they got to the doorway, they cocked their heads, looked at it for a moment, and scooted away.

"You'd think there was a chopping block in there," Mama said, laughing.

Then she had another idea. She picked up two long straight branches, and found two long straight branches for Rose. Then they held the sticks out at their sides, dragging on the ground, to make it harder for the chickens to sneak by them.

Mama and Rose patiently herded the chickens into a little crowd using those sticks. The nervous chickens walked around each other in circles, cackling, squawking, and flapping their wings. They milled noisily in front of the henhouse's little door.

But still they refused to go in.

"Well, that does it," Mama said, throwing away the sticks. "If we get them too riled up, they won't lay for weeks. Maybe they need a day or so to get accustomed to it."

In a few minutes, all the chickens had flown up into the roosting tree.

The next day, Mama left the henhouse doors open. She spread more cornmeal on the floor of the henhouse and set the water bowl nearby. The hens went into the henhouse and ate all the cornmeal. They drank the water. But near roosting time, they marched out of the henhouse and flew up into the tree.

Every night Mama and Rose tried to herd the chickens using the sticks. A few chickens went into the henhouse through the big door. So Mama locked them in for the night.

The next night, a few more chickens went in, and the rest flew up into the tree.

Finally, one evening, all the chickens let Mama and Rose herd them into the henhouse.

For a long time after that, the hens did a funny thing: When anyone picked up a long stick, or carried the broom, they scurried to the henhouse.

Mama's Window

The green of the oak leaves began to fade. The sumac trees along Fry Creek turned impossibly, brilliantly red. Rose noticed one day that the hickory leaves had turned yellow. More and more acorns fell from the oak tree next to the house. When the wind blew, the wooden roof tapped and rattled with the sound of acorns falling and rolling. It sounded like little animals were scampering about up there.

Brown and yellow leaves drifted down like a soft, crinkly rain. Rose liked walking through the soft crunchy piles that gathered along the house and against the tree trunks.

The air was full of butterflies, too. There were small bright-yellow ones and many that were black and orange. Rose often mistook them for fluttering leaves. Black butterflies with shimmering blue and white spots sat on the last flowers of summer and slowly waved their wings.

When Rose stepped outside to gather stove wood one morning, the forest was hidden behind a curtain of thick cottony fog. She had never seen anything so strange. The woods were perfectly still. She could hear the horses whinnying for their breakfast, and Papa's voice answering them. She could hear the chickens clucking. But she could not see anything beyond the nearest tree.

Everything was wet. A slow rain of fog water dripped off the dying oak leaves and the tree limbs. Water from the fog dripped lazily from the roof.

After breakfast, the sun began to burn through. Then Rose noticed something else. During the night, spiders had woven webs everywhere. There were spiderwebs draped on the grass stems, like tiny lace tablecloths. There were webs around the edges of the roof. Webs clung to the wagon spokes. Spiders had spun them in the bushes and in the trees and even in the curled-up, dried-out blossoms of Queen Anne's lace.

Each silky thread was strung with rows of tiny water beads, left there by the fog. Each silvery web had a fat yellow-striped spider perched in the middle. Rose worried the spiders with a stick until they scrambled off to the side.

When the sun finally burned through the fog, its yellow rays struck the webs and set them sparkling like jeweled necklaces. Rose looked up close: Each water bead had a tiny golden sun in it that glittered with the colors of a rainbow.

By midmorning, the sun had dried out all the webs. By dinner, Rose could not find any webs or any spiders. Then, the next morning, they were there all over again.

Mornings were chilly now. When Rose

sleepily stretched an arm out from under her patchwork quilt, the air felt as cool as the water in the spring.

"Time to chink the cabin," Papa said, shivering as he pulled on his shoes.

He went to the creek right after breakfast the next morning and brought back a bucket of reddish-brown clay. All around the outside of the house he stuffed and hammered chips of wood into the spaces between the logs. Then he smeared clay around the chips, to seal up the holes.

"Can I help, Papa?" Rose asked.

"Of course you can," said Papa. "Why didn't I think of it? You plug the holes down at the bottom. I'll do the ones up high."

Together they smeared clay into all those holes and cracks between the logs. Rose enjoyed the smooth feel of the clay, and she tried hard to do a tidy job.

When Papa looked to see how she was doing, he surprised her by bursting out with a great hearty laugh.

"Why, you're as dirty as a mud fence after a

rain," he said, brushing a bit of dried clay from her cheek. "But look what a fine job you're doing. Nothing can get through those cracks now."

When they were done, the little log house was warm and cozy. But now it was very dark, especially with the door closed.

"It's a sin to burn coal oil in the daytime," Mama said. "But I can barely see what I'm doing."

So Papa sent Cyrus into Mansfield to deliver a load of wood and came to the house with his ax, hammer, and chisel.

"Oh, Manly. You'll cut the window right now?" Mama said. "How wonderful! Let's see, I made a mark on the logs. Right here, on the west wall. That way I can see the sunset when I'm inside preparing for supper or kneading dough."

"Very well, Bess," said Papa. "Like the good Lord said, Let there be light."

First, he measured out a square, two logs high, on the outside of the wall and marked it with scratch lines. Then he hammered a deep cut with the chisel along the scratch lines.

Next he chopped out a log with the ax. While Papa chopped from the outside, Rose ran inside so she could see the moment there was a hole. For the longest time there was nothing but the sound of Papa's ax thunking into the wood. Then the shiny edge of the ax blade poked through the wood, and then wiggled, as Papa pulled it out. It poked and wiggled, poked and wiggled.

Finally a sliver of daylight appeared. Chips flew into the cabin. Papa kept chopping until he had cut all the way through, on both ends of the width he had marked on the log. He pushed, and a section of log fell into the house with a great clunk. Now there was a real hole in the wall, with Papa's face peering through it.

Rose got the broom to sweep up the chips.

"Not yet," Mama said. "Papa isn't done."

Papa took Cyrus' two-handled saw and pushed it through the hole. Mama took the other end, and together they pushed and pulled until they had made a clean, straight cut all the way through the log below. Then they did the same thing at the other end of the log.

The second piece of log fell into the house, *clunk!*

Now the hole was as big as a window in a sawed-board house. Light and fresh air poured into the room. Rose could see the wagon tracks going down toward Fry Creek. They wouldn't have to go outside to see if company was coming. Mama would know just when to put supper on the table when Papa came home.

The light also let them see all the corners inside the house. "I've got to get my broom in those rafters," Mama said. "The spiders have filled them with new webs."

At dinner they all looked out the window as they ate, watching the leaves fluttering and the birds flitting by.

"Windows are like pictures," Mama said. "Only better. They're never the same for two hours together."

In the afternoon Papa made the windowframe from hewn boards. He made auger holes in the boards and in the logs, two on either side and two each in the top and the bottom. He whittled eight wooden pegs with his knife and hammered them through the boards into the logs, good and snug.

Papa measured the windowframe carefully, and when Cyrus returned, he rode into town. He came back carrying a piece of glass in a wooden frame. Two shiny brass hinges were attached to one edge. He set that frame inside the one he had built and attached the hinges. Now it was a real window that opened and closed. Finally, Papa made a leather catch so the window could be shut tight.

Then they stood back to admire it.

"It's just beautiful!" said Mama. "The house seems bigger, and friendlier."

Rose looked out the window through the trees. So many leaves had fallen that she could see all the way to the little valley now. Very slowly, without Rose having noticed, winter was coming.

A *Walk in the Woods*

Each day was full of chores. It was Rose's chore to make sure there was enough cookwood by the stove. She peeled potatoes, or sorted beans, or stirred cornmeal. She set the table before meals and helped wash and dry the dishes after. Then she put them away in the dish box, all except the bread plate. Rose was too short to reach the mantel, where it belonged.

She swept the cabin and made her trundle bed. Then she pushed it away, under the big bed.

She carried buckets of water for the chickens, for the horses, for cooking, for laundry, for the washbasin, for the dishes, for housecleaning, for Saturday baths, and for drinking. She fed the chickens and hunted eggs. Once a week, she helped Mama clean the soiled leaves out of the henhouse. Then they put down a bed of fresh ones.

On Mondays, Rose helped Mama wash the clothes. She stirred the big tin basin full of steaming-hot water. She wasn't strong enough to scrub their dresses and Papa's overalls. But she could scrub the socks. Then she helped rinse everything, three times, and hang it to dry. On Tuesdays, she helped Mama with ironing. On Fridays, they cleaned the whole house, rafters to floors. On Saturdays, Mama baked bread. Rose helped mix the dough.

In between there was mending and sewing. And Rose had her lessons.

There was hardly time left over for playing, except on Sundays. They still got up early to do their morning chores. The horses had to be fed and watered, no matter what day it was. The chickens still must be pampered. Stove wood must be gathered.

But after breakfast, and after Mama had read to them from the Bible, Papa napped, Mama wrote, and Rose read one of Mama's poetry books. A fire crackled on the hearth; the air was rich with the smell of Sunday dinner cooking on the stove. They were safe and snug in their little log house.

But Rose was lonely. She missed having someone to play with. She missed Paul and George.

When she got restless, she went outside and played fetch with Fido. She poked around in the woods and looked for Indian arrowheads by the creek.

One Sunday Papa said she could scratch Pet's chest. So Rose took a corncob and walked across the clearing to where Papa kept the horses tied. She pulled up some grass and let Prince nibble it from her hand.

She heard a noise and looked up. A girl was walking up the wagon track. She was wearing a boy's straw hat. Peeking out from under the hat was a pigtail, fiery red.

"Alva!" Rose called out.

"Say, Rose!" Alva shouted. "I'm going to see a deer rub. Come on, I'll show you."

"Deer rub?" said Rose. "What's that?"

"You never seen a deer either?" Alva said. "Well, come on then. Maybe we'll see one."

Mama said hello to Alva and told Rose she must be back in time for dinner. Rose and Alva walked a long, long way from the farm. They walked along streams, climbed hills, and explored little valleys. On the way, Alva showed Rose the forest.

They walked along a little stream between two hills. Alva stopped suddenly and pointed at the water: "Look, a crawdad!"

Rose saw a smoky cloud of stirred-up mud in the stream. Alva knelt down, staring intently at something. She reached out her hand, very slowly and carefully.

Fido watched, his head cocked to one side.

Suddenly, Alva's hand darted into the water. Fido barked excitedly. In a second Alva was holding something right in front of Rose's face.

It was an ugly brown creature, big as a

baby's foot, dripping wet, and wriggling to get free. Its bulgy eyes came out of its head on stalks. Its two rows of little legs squirmed and crawled in the air. Its scaly tail curled and snapped.

Alva held it behind its head. Its two front legs had claws on them, snapping at the air, trying to pinch Rose.

"It's trying to bite!" Rose said.

"Watch this," said Alva. She picked up a little twig and held it in front of the wriggling crawdad. The creature reached out with one of its claws and cut the little twig in two!

Then Alva threw it back into the stream. It vanished so quickly, no eye could follow it.

"They're good to eat," Alva said. "Of a day, we ought to catch ourselves a mess in Fry Creek and cook 'em up."

They came to a grove of small trees. The bark on some of them had been rubbed off in streaks. That was a deer rub, Alva said.

"The deer comes and rubs his baby horns, to make them strong."

But they didn't see any deer.

Alva showed Rose raccoon tracks, which looked like a child's handprints. She showed her holes in the ground where foxes slept. Fido crisscrossed the woods. He stuck his nose into rotting logs and fox dens and raccoon tracks.

Alva showed Rose tracks where civet cats had walked in the mud. A civet cat was like a skunk, Alva said. "Only they ain't so waddly. And you don't get much for the fur."

Alva knew about all the forest creatures. She knew about hunting. She knew about trapping. Alva even had her own money that she earned from trapping and selling the furs.

"I got seventy cents all saved up from selling pelts," Alva said. "You can come to my house and look at it. My ma says to keep it, for when I get married. But I don't know if I will. If I was an old maid, I could stay with my pa and get my own gun."

Alva also told Rose a panther story:

"One time it was real hot and this mama and papa went to sleep with their door open, to get the air," she began. "A panther sneaked into the house and stole the little baby right out of the mama's arms, when she was sleeping." Alva's eyes were big and round, and she spoke in a whisper, as if the trees might hear. "That big old cat was so sneaky, the mama didn't hear nothing till the baby started screaming.

"All the menfolk got together and hunted that panther to its den. Then they waited for it to come out. They waited the longest time— days, it was. Pointing their guns and just waiting. That old panther knew they was waiting, too.

"Finally he got so hungry, he come running out of his den, screaming the most horrible scream, like a madwoman. That's what they sound like. The men shot it dead, right there and then. They never did find that poor little baby. Except a hunk of its dress, was all."

Rose couldn't tell if Alva had made up that story or not. "I think I should go home now," she said, looking around. "It must be almost dinner. We aren't lost, are we?"

"You won't never get lost, long as you're around me," Alva bragged. "I know my way in these hills better'n anybody. But I'll tell you a little secret: If you get lost, walk downhill."

"Downhill?" said Rose.

"And keep going downhill," Alva said. "Pretty soon you'll come to a creek, or a fence, or maybe a farm. Then you ain't lost no more!"

Rabbit Stew

On the way back to Rocky Ridge, Alva told Rose, "There's plenty you ain't seen yet. Come winter, I'll take you around my trap line. You ought to get your pa to stick a rabbit gum around here, Rose. There's always rabbits hiding in them brush piles."

Rose remembered Fido's sniffing. "What's a rabbit gum?"

"A kind of trap," said Alva. "You can make one from a hollow black gum log. But just for fun, sometimes you can scare the rabbits out by jumping up and down on top of the pile."

The faraway sound of a bell floated on the breeze. "There's my ma, calling dinner. I got to go."

"Good-bye," Rose shouted out as Alva ran down the hill. Alva was different from any girl Rose had ever met. She was much more fun than the polite girls Rose had played with in De Smet. Alva told wonderfully scary stories. And she was very smart.

At dinner, Rose told Mama and Papa all about the walk. They listened to every word. Mama's eyes grew as Rose repeated Alva's panther story.

"I don't like panthers," said Mama. "I remember the time one almost jumped on Pa, when I was a little girl. The sound of its cry was awful."

After dinner, Rose went outside to play. She circled the brush pile, looking at it. She knew she had to try climbing it. Rose put her foot on a jutting tree limb. The pile leaned unsteadily as her feet searched for solid places to stand. Branches snapped under her, sending her legs plunging into the tangle. But finally she was perched on the very top, straddling two branches, as high as the wagon-box.

The brush pile was very springy. Rose bounced up and down, a little at first. The whole pile bounced under her. Sticks and limbs crackled. Rose bounced higher, and higher, until the whole pile was bouncing.

Suddenly a rabbit darted out one side of the pile and bounded away into a bush at the edge of the woods.

"Fido!" Rose shouted. But Fido was nowhere to be seen. Rose clambered down as fast as she could and ran after it.

She picked up a stick and beat the bush. The rabbit leaped out and ran up the hill. Rose chased the rabbit up and down the hill, through bushes, and over rocks. Every time the rabbit stopped, Rose scared it up again.

Soon she was just about out of breath. Her feet hurt from stubbing them on rocks. But the rabbit was tired, too. When Fido finally came running, the rabbit hopped into a hollow log.

Rose got down on her hands and knees to

look. She could see the shadow of its head and ears. Fido whined and wagged his tail furiously. He wanted to get into the log, but it narrowed too much in the middle.

Rose found a big rock nearby that she pushed and rolled over to the log. She pushed it into one end. Then she found another rock and pushed and rolled it against the other end. Now she had really caught that rabbit! She shrieked with delight. Fido pawed and whined.

Then Rose asked herself, "Now what?"

Papa would know what to do. She raced back to the log house to fetch him.

"He's in there pretty far," Papa said when Rose showed him the log. He found a stick and, with his knife, he split the end of it. Then he pushed the split end into the log, as far as it would go. He twisted it and twisted it. Then he tugged on the stick. Something was pulling against him. Then out came the rabbit, its fur tangled up in the split end of the stick. It was kicking hard.

"Whoops!" Papa shouted, reaching to grab

the rabbit by the neck.

But the rabbit gave one mighty kick against Papa's leg. It bounded free of the stick and out of his hands. Fido leaped up. Right in midair, he caught the rabbit by its neck and gave it one mighty shake.

That night the family sat down to Sunday supper of corn bread and rabbit stew. Fido got his share, too. "My little prairie Rose is becoming quite the woodsman," said Papa.

"Yes, Rose," Mama agreed. "That rabbit was so plump, there will be gravy enough for tomorrow's dinner."

But Rose did not feel like a woodsman. And even though she was very hungry, she ate just her corn bread.

"You've hardly touched your supper," Mama finally said. "Are you ill?"

"No," Rose said quietly. "I'm not very hungry."

"I'm surprised at you, Rose. You've liked rabbit stew when I've made it before."

Papa looked at Rose thoughtfully for a moment. Then he laid down his fork and wiped his mustache on his napkin. "Come here," he said gently. Rose went and sat on his knee. "You know, your capturing that rabbit was a lucky stroke for us."

"It was?" said Rose.

"Yes indeed," said Papa. "We must all keep up our strength, to work this farm and build it. And every meal we harvest from our own land is a lucky stroke, because it is a meal we don't have to earn by cutting, hauling, and selling wood. That rabbit you caught is helping to keep us free and independent, Rose. So long as we can live off our land, we will never be beholden to others."

Then Mama asked, "Do you remember what it says in the Bible about harvesting?"

"What?"

"It says, 'To every thing there is a season: a time to plant, and a time to pluck that which is planted.' It was time to pluck up that rabbit, Rose. To harvest its life, to nourish and sustain our own. You can be proud that you helped feed this family."

Rose had never thought of rabbits as a harvest, like wheat. Alva knew it. Now Rose did too.

She went back to her dinner and by the last bite Rose remembered how much she liked Mama's rabbit stew. Wait till she told Alva about that rabbit!

One morning, Papa and Cyrus hitched the horses and began dragging logs from a great pile they had cut to a place across the clearing from the house. There they began to build the barn.

First they laid logs on the ground to make two big squares, with a space between. Those were the sills. The space between the two big squares was where Papa would store the harness and wagon.

After dinner Papa sent Cyrus into town to deliver wood. "Think I'll check on the orchard," Papa said.

Rose was stirring laundry in the tub in front of the house, and Mama was hanging up rinsed things, when Papa came running. Without a word he ran into the house. Mama ran in after him. "Manly, what—?"

Then they both came right back out again. Papa had his rifle, and Mama had the broom. "Stay here, Rose," Mama said, and off they dashed.

But Rose couldn't obey. She snatched a branch off the ground and ran after them. She followed them around the hill behind the spring. She caught up with them in the orchard. Papa was running around the little apple trees, shouting madly, "Go on! Scoot! Get gone! Ho! Hey!"

Fido was barking wildly at a brush pile. Rose looked more closely. A huge animal was lurking behind it. She could see its black body moving, but she couldn't see what it was.

Mama walked up to the brush pile. Fido dashed around the other side. Suddenly, out rushed an enormous black hog! It was snorting loudly and running hard. It was rushing straight at Mama!

"Mama, look out!" Rose screamed.

Mama raised the broom to hit the hog on the snout. But just then Fido ran up behind it and sank his sharp teeth into the hog's hind leg. The hog squealed horribly and whirled on little Fido, snapping. Rose could hear its vicious teeth clicking.

"Look out!" Rose shrieked again.

The hog kicked and whirled. It squealed and snapped. But Fido was too nimble and quick. He whirled with it, his teeth sunk fast in the hog's leg. The hog could not hurt him.

Finally Fido let go. The hog rushed off into the woods. They could hear it crashing through the bushes for a long time after it was out of sight.

Papa came back, breathing hard. "I think I scared the rest of them off," he said. "Must be a sow. There was a bunch of smaller pigs, too. They were stripping the bark right off the apple trees. They ruined a whole row before I caught them."

"Now what?" said Mama. "We can't shoot them. Surely they belong to some farmer."

"I'm certain they do," said Papa. "Missouri has free-range laws. A farmer can let his hogs run wild, even on someone else's land, until he's ready to go find and butcher them. Each farmer notches his hogs' ears with a special mark, to tell whose hog is whose."

"I never heard of such an outlandish law," said Mama. "What are we supposed to do, just let them chew up our orchard?"

"Not on your tintype," said Papa. "We'll have to build a fence around the apple trees. The barn will wait."

"I declare," said Mama. "It's always something else, isn't it?"

"That's life," Papa said, wiping his brow. "If it isn't chickens, it's feathers."

Stubborn Land

Mama's excited voice woke Rose up.

"Oh, Manly," she said from the lean-to doorway. "I've never seen anything so lovely."

Rose flung back her quilt and jumped out of bed. The wooden floor was cold. She hugged herself as she ran to the doorway and squeezed between Mama and Papa.

"What is it?" she demanded, rubbing the sleep from her eyes.

Every tree, every limb, every single leaf and blade of grass, the house, the henhouse, the wagon—everything in the whole outside world—wore a coat of silvery white. The silvered trees looked like white lace. The frosted henhouse looked like a cake that had been dusted with powdered sugar.

"You couldn't dream a world so beautiful," Mama said.

"What did that?" Rose asked.

"It's the hoarfrost," said Papa. "It comes when the fog freezes."

Rose walked out onto the frosty ground. The bottoms of her feet felt like a hundred tiny needles were poking them. She picked a blade of grass. It was covered with a delicate fur of ice crystals. When she touched it with her tongue, the fur melted. Everything in sight shimmered with it. Here and there a breeze blew a puff of it from a branch. It drifted away like silver dust.

The hoarfrost brought a hush to the woods, too. The birds were too surprised to sing.

When Rose opened the little door, the chickens poked their heads out and blinked in the brightness. They clucked nervously. Their little beaks puffed tiny breaths of steam. The chickens were too cozy to come out and walk on the frozen fog.

Steam rose from the spring like a column of chimney smoke. Mist floated over Fry Creek.

"I'd better plow up the garden plot today," Papa said. "Before the ground freezes."

"At least make room for peas and potatoes," said Mama. "Those will be the first to go in."

The only open land Rose had seen on Rocky Ridge was waiting for the apple trees. In South Dakota all the land was open. Now they lived in the forest.

"Where can we plant a garden, Papa?" Rose asked.

"Right out there," he said, pointing to the woods. "It's just waiting to be plowed."

Papa drove the wagon to borrow Mr. Stubbins' plow. He hitched the mares to it and began to break the stony ground between the trees.

It was a strange thing to see. Even Mama chuckled at the sight of a man driving a plow through the woods. But Papa said he didn't have to cut all those trees down. He would deaden them by chopping the bark off in a ring, all the way around the trunk. In the spring, no leaves would sprout, and sunlight could pour down through the bare limbs onto the garden.

"In a few years, the dead trees will rot and fall," Papa explained. It was a way a man could clear land without having to cut trees and pull out stumps.

But Rose and Mama did not laugh long. The plow point kept striking hidden rocks and tree roots. Each time, the plow handle jerked to a stop and Papa stumbled in the lines.

Rose cringed at the sound of the horses grunting as the harness dug into their necks. The shock of the sudden stops knocked the breath from them in clouds of steam. They pawed in frustration. They could not see what was holding them back.

Papa spoke to the horses. The mares strained to obey him. They tried as hard as they could to tear the plow point through those roots, but they couldn't do it.

"What is it?" Mama called out anxiously.

"Stubbins told me this might be a problem," Papa said. "It takes mules to break this soil. I see what he meant. It takes a stubborn mule to fight a stubborn land."

Papa got the ax and chopped the roots through. Then he put his shoulders into the lines again and chirruped to the horses. But a hidden rock tossed the plow aside. Another one threw it up out of the ground. Mama helped Papa dig up the heavy rocks and throw them out of the way.

Then the plow point hit another root. But this time, Papa fell onto the end of the plow handle. He moaned as the handle punched him in the stomach. Mama gasped as Papa crumpled to the ground.

"Oh, Manly!" Mama cried out.

"Papa!" cried Rose.

They ran to his side. Mama bent over him. Rose heard him gasping. Her eyes welled up with tears.

"Rose, dampen a cloth and bring it here, quick!" Mama said.

Rose couldn't budge. She stared at Papa,

rocking on the ground. She had never seen such pain in his face.

"It's all right, Rose," Mama said. "Papa just had his breath knocked out of him. Now run and get that cloth."

Fear gave Rose extra speed. But it also made her clumsy. She tripped on the doorsill and knocked over a chair. She snatched a dish towel from the handle of the bucket, dunked it in the water, and ran back.

Papa was sitting up. His face was pale, but he smiled weakly at her. She threw her arms around his neck and hugged him hard.

"There, Rose. Don't cry," Papa said. "It's just a little accident."

Mama helped Papa limp to bed. Then she unhitched the team. Afterward she made him a cup of tea. Papa stayed in bed the rest of the day with a stomachache.

"I'll have to borrow a pair of mules," he said. "I can't wear out the horses that way."

"I'll thank you to be more careful after this," said Mama, putting wood on the fire. "My heart was in my mouth."

Papa borrowed Mr. Stubbins' mules and finished plowing up the garden. But the land fought back every inch. Even the big-footed, long-eared mules sometimes could not pull the plow through those roots. But they tried and tried.

"They are snappish and ugly," Papa said. "But I don't think you could ever wear a mule out."

After the plow had scarred the earth, Rose helped Mama pick up the rocks. For many days, all day long, they picked up rocks and threw them to the side of the garden. No matter how many rocks they took out, the earth grew more.

"I never saw anything like it," Mama said. "Just when I think I've cleared a piece of it, I turn around and there are more."

That was the hardest chore Rose had done yet. Her back ached from bending over. The stones chafed and cut her hands. Her arms and shoulders were sore. Her hands were cold and dirty.

But when they were done, Rose looked at

that garden with pride. The reddish-brown soil between the trees was all churned and clean, a fresh blanket of earth. In the spring, Papa would plow it again to break up the chunks. Then they would hoe it and tuck in the tiny seeds of their first garden.

In the spring they would plant their own corn. They would plant alfalfa, too, to feed the horses. They would plant the apple trees properly. But Mama said they would have to make do with what they had this winter. They would have to endure.

South Dakota was wheat country, and they had always had bread to eat. But wheat didn't grow in the Ozarks. At first Rose had enjoyed all that corn bread, covered with molasses. But it wasn't special anymore. In fact, she was growing tired of it. She missed milk, too.

In the morning Mama gave her a steaming bowl of brown beans, a cup of water—and a piece of corn bread. Without thinking, Rose sighed and made a face. As soon as she did it, she looked to see if Mama or Papa had noticed. Mama was tending the stove, her back turned. Papa was bending over, tying his shoes.

Rose's face burned with shame. It was sinful to want things she couldn't have.

Falling Behind

Papa pulled on his jacket after breakfast, picked up the ax, and was headed for the door when there was a knock.

"Who could that be?" Mama said. Fido hadn't barked and none of them had heard a wagon's rattle or the jingle of harness.

Papa opened the door. Cyrus stood there, his hat in his hand.

"Morning, Mr. Wilder," he said. "'Scuse me for busting in like this. But my wife and young'uns are down the creek, waiting in the wagon. We're moving on. Something came up, just that quick.

"So I came to tell you . . . well, you treated me square, is all. You're a man of your word, and I reckon the leastest way I can show my thanks is to shake your hand. We won't never forget what you done for us, sir."

Papa was so stunned, he forgot for a moment to meet Cyrus' handshake. Mama just stood there, the half-washed plate in her hands dripping on the floor. Rose placed the cup she had just dried in the dish box. It settled with a noisy clatter that startled her.

"Yes, of course," Papa finally said, taking Cyrus' hand. "I wondered how much longer you'd camp there, with cold weather due. You found a situation then?"

"My brother down Eureka Springs way sent for me," Cyrus said. "There's steady work for carpenters. Sounds like it's a boom town. Folks coming from all over, to take the healing waters and all. Being it's winter and out of season, we'll find us a reasonable roof over our heads till spring."

"I'm sorry to see you go, Cyrus. But we wish you well," Papa said. "If ever you're by this way, give a shout."

"Yessir," said Cyrus. "I'll do it. Good luck."

Papa watched him walk down the hill. Then he closed the door and came back inside. Mama sat down heavily.

"I worried about this," Papa said, laying down the ax.

Mama sighed. "We won't get the barn up in time for winter now."

"I don't see how," said Papa. "Those hogs were tearing up the orchard again last week. I have to finish that fence before anything. We might get a mild winter. Then the horses could stay out. I could build a shelter between some trees and fence it in. But if the weather's bad, I've got to stable them in town."

"But Manly, how could we possibly pay for it?" Mama asked. "The chickens are nearly done laying until spring. With Cyrus gone, how can you cut and sell enough wood to make ends meet?"

"We own a farm, Bess," Papa replied. "We've got near a thousand apple trees, and good timber, and four healthy horses. We can get credit in town anytime we need."

"I don't like it. There must be another way," Mama said. Her hands balled into fists. "We'll need credit for spring planting as it is, for seed and supplies. I hate for us to start all over again slaving to fatten merchants and bankers. We came all this way to break that cycle of debt. Once you fall behind, you never catch up. It's every farmer's ruination."

Rose dried the last dishes as quietly as she could.

"It's not as bad as all that, Bess," Papa said. "Remember, we've got all the firewood we could ever need, right at our doorstep. In Dakota, coal to last the winter cost us a hundred dollars. That's a big saving right there. And spring comes a month, maybe two months earlier here. We'll have our harvesting done that much sooner."

Mama got up and carried the washbasin outside to empty the dirty water. Papa hung up his jacket.

When she came back in, Mama's face was set. "I lack the strength to lift logs," she said, folding the dish towel. "And I certainly know nothing about building a barn," she added, untying her apron. "But I've got my two hands, I've driven a team, and I can work as hard as the day is long. Let's get down to the woodlot, Manly. We've wasted enough daylight as it is."

So Mama went to work helping Papa. The sharp ax was too heavy for her to swing. But Papa bought a two-handled saw and she could hold one end of it, to help Papa cut logs into stove wood and fence lengths. Then Papa split the logs, some into stove wood and others into fence rails. Mama helped carry the rails to the orchard and lay them in place.

Rose had extra chores now. Mama taught her how to make the fire for dinner and supper. Rose tidied the house by herself after breakfast. She even made the big bed, although she could never seem to get the quilt to hang perfectly straight.

When her morning chores were done, Rose watched Mama and Papa in the wood lot. She picked up stove wood that Papa had split and stacked it neatly. Rose was watching Mama and Papa pushing and pulling the saw when Mama's hands slipped off the handle in the middle of a pull. Mama lost her balance and sat down hard on the ground with an "Oomph!"

Mama's legs stuck out from her dress, like a doll's. Her hair had come undone and she was red in the face. Rose couldn't help laughing. Papa's mouth twitched at the corners, and then he guffawed loudly. He went to Mama and helped her to her feet.

"I'm sorry, Bess," he said. "Are you all right?"

"If my pa could see me now," Mama said, "he'd be laughing louder than either of you. I'm just fine." She brushed the leaves and sawdust from her skirt. Then the rasping of the saw began again.

The days of work were even longer than before. When supper was over, they climbed into their soft beds and slept deeply until the nickel-plated alarm clock woke them in the dark, and it was time to start all over again.

Cave

No matter how much work there was to do, they still rested on Sundays.

"I miss going to church," Mama told Papa. "Especially the music. But I can't decide which one. I lean toward Presbyterian, but I'd hate to go to one and find I preferred the other. I don't want to offend either."

"We could wait and see what the Cooleys learn," said Papa. "After all, they live right in town."

"Yes," said Mama. "Do ask them next time you see them."

Some Sundays Alva came to visit. She and

Rose played in the woods or down at the creek. They made little houses out of rocks. They dammed up the spring branch to make a little pond. They hunted for crawdads and ate ripe persimmons.

One Sunday Alva showed Rose a cave. It was an enormous hole in the side of a hill near the farm. The hole went deep into the hill. Dead ferns lined the top of the opening. A little stream trickled out of it and wandered away into the woods. From inside that great hole, Rose heard the hollow sound of dripping water. Musty air flowed from its great mouth.

"What's in there?" Rose asked.

"Things you ain't never seen," Alva said. "Crickets that look like bumblebees. Bats. And sometimes hogs."

"Hogs?" said Rose. She had seen hogs in the orchard and didn't want to meet one anywhere.

"Yep," said Alva. "They live in caves sometimes. They're mean, too. A mean old hog could kill a dog easy."

"Are there hogs in there now?"

"Probably not," said Alva. "If any hogs are living here, they're out eating acorns. Come on," she said, walking through the opening. "Do you want to see or not? It's nothing to be afraid of. I come here plenty." Her voice turned hollow-sounding as they walked into a dark, empty room with a high ceiling. The air was warmer inside.

"It makes your voice echo," said Rose, hearing the hollow sound of her own voice. "Hello!" she shouted, and from somewhere inside the cave came a tiny answer, "Hello." Her voice sounded very big in there.

"Listen to this," said Alva, and she screamed at the top of her lungs. The cave made her voice so enormous and scary-sounding that Rose just had to scream along with her. Then they both laughed until they were senseless.

Finally they were quiet again. The sound of falling water was louder now. The floor was covered with rocks and stones. They walked a little farther in, around a corner. Light from the cave opening showed water raining from a crack in the ceiling onto the stones below.

"Come on," Alva said. "If them hogs was here, they'd of showed theirselves. Or you'd of smelled them. There ain't no hog tracks, anyway."

The cave grew smaller and became a long narrow tunnel, just tall enough for them to stand up. The light from outside grew dimmer as it struggled to reach around the bends.

A little stream ran down the middle of the tunnel. The water was icy on their bare feet, so Alva and Rose walked on a muddy ledge that ran beside the stream. Their feet made sucking, smacking sounds when they picked them up. The rough stone wall felt cool and damp when Rose touched it. The air smelled clammy.

They walked until they could not see anything in front of them. Rose stared into the blackness. There was nothing for the eye to rest on. She couldn't even see her hand, or the wall right by her head. There was only pure darkness that seemed to swallow her up.

"I can't see anything," Rose said. Now her voice sounded small and muffled, as if the walls were soaking it up. "I think we should go back."

She turned around and was shocked to see the light from the cave's mouth far behind them. It was just a small pale smudge in the distance. It was very quiet there, too.

SPLASH!

"What was that!" Rose shouted. "Did you do that?"

"Not me," Alva said in a quivery voice.

Rose's legs prickled with fear.

They stood still, staring into the blackness, listening to the silence.

Then they heard it again: *SPLASH*, then *splash-splash-splash*, *splish*. They heard a grunt.

"Uh-oh," Alva said.

Without another thought, Rose spun and ran. She didn't care about the cold water now. She ran wherever her feet landed. She heard Alva running behind her. She felt splashes of water from Alva's running feet.

Rose did not stop to look. The sound of their footsteps slapping and sucking in the mud, and the splashing and thrashing in the water, echoed on the stone walls, chasing her like some wild animal. She tripped and fell, scraping her hands on the rocks. Alva flew past.

Rose got up and ran even faster until finally she burst into the opening. She had to squint against the brilliant sunlight pouring down on the forest outside.

Rose kept running until she caught up to Alva. She was doubled over, trying to catch her breath. Rose collapsed on the ground. She gulped in the fresh dry air. It smelled sweet and clean after the musty dampness of the cave. The woods were peaceful and safe.

Rose's legs trembled. Her lungs burned. Her palms were raw from the fall. But she laughed from relief. She looked back toward the cave, held her breath, and listened. But all she could hear was the sound of trickling water in the stream coming from the cave, and the cawing of crows quarreling with each other in the tall trees.

"What was that sound?" asked Rose. "Was it a hog?"

"Naw," Alva said. "Maybe a bobcat or a raccoon. Raccoons like to splash in the water."

They washed the mud off their hands and dresses and walked back to the farm. As scared as she had been, Rose thought the cave was the most exciting thing Alva had showed her so far.

Barn Raising

We are falling behind," Papa repeated one night at supper. "The fence is done but we can't cut enough wood, just the two of us, to keep going. I need to take a job in town."

Papa was sitting by the chimney place. He stretched his long legs out on the hearth and filled a corncob pipe. The good smell of tobacco mixed with the scent of burning hickory logs in the fireplace.

Mama was sitting at the table mending a hole in Rose's winter coat. "Must you?" she said.

"Just for now, Bess. John Cooley told me of a job driving a wagon, delivering coal oil. He says it's mine for the asking, and I aim to ask."

Mama was quiet for a long time after that.

"The first mortgage payment is due next month," she finally said.

"We'll scrape by," said Papa.

"And the barn? What about the horses?"

"Let me think about that one a spell," said Papa. "I have an idea."

Papa rode off each morning to town, to drive another man's wagon. He came home at night, smelling of coal oil. Mama had to wash his overalls every day to get out the odor. He also sold or traded the asbestos fire mats.

"You see, Bess, I told you those things would pay for themselves," Papa said when they were all gone. "They earned us one whole dollar, without our lifting a finger."

"Just you remember, we're farmers, not merchants," said Mama.

One morning, after Papa left, Mama told Rose they were going to clean the house, top to bottom.

"It isn't Friday yet," Rose said.

"Company's coming," said Mama. "The Cooleys and Alva's family."

Rose was surprised. "Paul and George? And Alva? Everyone is coming here?"

"Yes," said Mama. "They are coming to help finish the barn, and I want the place to shine. We may not live like nabobs, but that's no excuse for an untidy house."

"What's a nabob?"

"Never mind," Mama said. "Here's a rag. Start dusting the logs."

Mama took the broom and knocked the spiderwebs out of the rafters. After the dusting was done, they hung the rag rug outside, and Rose beat the dirt out of it with a stick.

They took the beds apart and fluffed up the straw ticks. Mama hung the quilts and sheets outside to air while they scrubbed the floor with sand, then rinsed it with water.

After dinner they cooked. Mama baked extra corn bread and rolled out pie crusts. Rose peeled enough apples for two pies, being careful to keep the peels thin so nothing would go to waste. Then Mama butchered her two oldest hens for a chicken pie she would make in the morning.

All day long Rose thought about the things she would show Paul and George.

And she couldn't wait to hear about living in the hotel.

Just before supper, Rose cleaned the lamp chimney and Mama dusted the face of the clock. Mama put their best quilt on the bed, the one with the red bear-claw pattern. She got out her second-best calico dress and Rose's blue school dress.

"There," Mama said, slumping tiredly into a chair. "I'm all done in. But the house is ready at least."

After the supper dishes were washed, they took baths and climbed wearily into bed. But it felt as if Rose had no sooner laid her head down than the alarm clock woke her up.

"Time to get up, Rose," Mama said. "We still have regular chores before everybody gets here."

Papa fed and watered the horses and got

them in harness. Rose rolled out crusts for the chicken pie.

They ate a cold breakfast so Mama could make the pie. She browned the pieces of chicken in salt pork and laid them in the spider-legged skillet. Then she sprinkled bits of salt pork and hard-boiled egg on them, and poured gravy over it all. Finally, she laid on the top crust, cut two pine trees in the dough, and set the skillet in the fireplace. It would be ready for dinner.

Rose swept out the cabin again, and then everything was ready. The eastern sky was just turning rosy when Fido barked: Mr. and Mrs. Cooley were driving up the hill in their wagon. Right behind them came a second wagon, with Alva on the seat between her mother and father.

"Say, Rose!" Paul shouted.

"Hello, Laura!" Mrs. Cooley cried out.

"Hello!" "Howdy!" "Aren't you a sight for sore eyes!" Everyone talked at once.

Rose was bursting with excitement. But she barely had time to say hello when she heard more wagon wheels ringing on the rocks. Another wagon was coming up the hill Behind it was still another. And another! Mama stared in wonderment. Papa whistled low.

"Well, I'll be starched," he said.

Those wagons pulled right up into the clearing. Men and women and children began pouring out of them.

"Who are all these strangers?" Mama asked Papa, her eyes wide.

"I didn't mention it, Bess, because I didn't expect it. Stubbins said he might pass the word along to the neighbors. Seems he did, at that. I'd say they've come to help."

Mama shook her head in disbelief. "Praise be," she said quietly. "I don't know what to think. How will I ever feed them all?"

"They brought food, Mama," Rose said. "Look."

The women on the wagon seats were handing down baskets with white cloths over them. Children were carrying pitchers and bowls. They were bringing all that food to the house.

Now the clearing became a swirl of activity. Women wearing large bonnets and pleasant smiles came to introduce themselves to Mama.

"Howdy, Mrs. Wilder. I'm Mrs. Lockwood. Our place is just the other side of the tracks. Sure is a sweet little spot you got here. Is that your little girl? Why, she has the most beautiful blue eyes. I brought some of my pickles today. I'll just set them over there."

"I'm Lydia Bates," said another woman. "I don't mean to pry, but would you be joining us down at the Methodist church? Everyone says we have the best choir in town. We'd be pleased to have you folks some Sunday."

Mama smiled shyly and thanked everyone politely. But she still had a bewildered look on her face.

Rose heard hearty greetings everywhere. All those strangers knew each other.

Mrs. Cooley helped Mama decide where to set all the food.

"Isn't it wonderful, Laura?" she said. "I've never met such friendly folks as I have since we came to Missouri. It took a bit of getting used to at first. But I wouldn't have it any other way now."

Papa spoke with Mr. Cooley and Mr.

Stubbins to plan out the barn raising. Their breath made a mist in the morning chill. Coats came off and were flung on stumps. Sharp axes, resting in the ends of logs, waited to go to work.

Rose wanted to watch the barn being built and to play with her friends. But there was no time for any of that.

"Come here," Mama said. "We've got plenty to do if we're to feed everybody by dinnertime."

All morning Rose and Alva ran in and out of the house helping the women prepare dinner. The house was crammed full of people. Rose never quit smiling. She hardly saw Paul and George at all. They were with the other boys, helping the men and tending the horses.

Rose and Alva took turns stirring the iron pot of beans and salt pork that simmered over a pit fire outside. Mrs. Stubbins had brought potatoes, which they roasted in the ashes.

Other neighbors had brought sweet potatoes and salt pork and smoked ham and fried chicken and bowls of pickles and bowls of

sweet-and-tart corn relish. There were apple pies and persimmon puddings and doughnuts and gingerbread. There were pitchers of milk and apple cider and ginger water.

All morning Rose heard the sounds of logs crashing as the horses dragged them from the pile to the place where the barn sills lay on the ground. Men groaned and shouted as they lifted the logs into place. Axes rang out as other men slashed notches into the logs so they fit together as perfectly as a jigsaw puzzle.

First side logs were set in place. Next end logs. Then side logs again. Slowly but surely the barn walls began to rise.

The day warmed until it was almost summery. Piles of clouds floated in the deep-blue sky. The rasping of saws and thudding of axes didn't stop all morning. Then, finally, one of the women took a wooden spoon and beat the bottom of an empty pail as loud as she could. A great cheer went up from the men. It was noontime, and that was the dinner bell.

All the food was laid out on planks that had

been made into tables by laying them on stumps. The logs were covered with pans and platters, bowls and pitchers, forks, spoons, plates, and cups. The children waited at the side while the women served the men.

Rose introduced Alva to Paul and George.

"Where do you live?" Alva asked. "I never seen you around here before."

"We live in town," Paul said. "In the Mansfield Hotel. My pa and ma run it."

"Well, that's something," Alva said. "I never been inside a hotel. What's it like?"

"It's the best place I ever lived," said Paul. Rose was surprised to see how much taller and older he looked. "You see different people coming and going all day, getting on and off the trains or driving into town to trade.

"Pa sends me to meet the trains and the stagecoaches from Hartville and Ava. Look, Rose. Pa even gave me my own pocket watch."

Paul pulled a silver watch from his pants pocket and opened it. It was handsome and grown-up, with a locomotive engraved on the back.

"I greet the guests and carry their bags," he said, snapping the watch shut. "Sometimes they even give me a nickel tip!"

"Why?" asked Rose.

"For being helpful and polite, of course," Paul said. "I also have to keep the lamps filled with coal oil, and the stoves hot when it's cold. And sweep out the rooms. I help make up the beds, too." He made a face at that.

"But gosh, Rose," he said, brightening. "It's practically the middle of the whole world!"

The jingle of harness and the shouts of the men going back to work told them that it was time for the women and children to eat.

A Real Farm

After dinner Rose and Alva helped wash the dishes. All the leftover food was packed away and the dishes, platters, bowls, pots, and pans put back in their baskets. Then the women went to their wagons and brought back knitting and sewing. They all sat outside the house on logs and stumps, chatting and laughing. Mama said Rose could go watch the men work on the barn.

The barn walls were finished. The ends of the logs at each corner were bright yellow where they had been trimmed for a snug fit. Wood chips lay everywhere like golden snowflakes. Now the men were sitting and standing on top of the walls. They were putting up small logs to make rafters for the roof.

The heavy log hauling was done, so Paul and George could watch, too.

"Come on," Rose said to Alva. "Let's show them the apple trees. Wild hogs tried to eat the bark," she told Paul and George, "but we chased them away."

On the way to the orchard, Rose told them about the tarantula, and the rats that were in the house until Fido got rid of them. She told them about the cave. Alva told her panther story.

"It sounds like fun living on a farm," George said as they walked back. "I hate working in the kitchen all the time. We hardly ever get to play. You play all the time."

Rose knew better, but she didn't say a word.

"It's nice here, all right," Paul said. "But I still like town better."

The rest of the afternoon, in between trips to the spring to bring water to the horses, the children watched the roof go on. Papa helped hand the bright, rived-board shingles he and Cyrus had split to the men balancing on the rafters. They nailed the rived-board shingles in rows, beginning at the roof's edge. Row by row, they continued up the rafters toward the peak.

Finally, when it was nearly time to start evening chores, the last shingle had been nailed in place. The barn was finished!

Families put their baskets and sewing back in the wagons and hitched their teams. Rose was sorry to see everyone go.

"See you in school, I guess," Paul said. "It starts in two weeks, you know."

"I won't see you," said Rose, feeling even more sorry now. "I'm not going. Not until next year, I think."

"Why not?" asked Paul. "You're the best student there is. You beat me in every spell-down."

"I have to help Mama and Papa," Rose said. "To build up the farm. But Mama said we could visit on Sundays."

Mama and Papa went around to all the wagons and shook everyone's hand. "We can't thank you enough." "Please let us know if we can ever be of help." "Do stop by, anytime." It took a long time to thank all those people and say good-bye. One by one, the wagons rumbled off down the hill. Finally, the Cooleys were the only ones left.

"It was a delightful day," Mrs. Cooley said. "But Laura, we hardly had time to talk! I've missed you so."

"I've missed you too, Emma," said Mama. "Especially when I think of the peaceful Sundays we shared on the way here. Traveling in the wagons seems almost like a holiday compared to the work of building up a farm."

"I know what you mean," Mrs. Cooley replied. "I have seven sets of sheets to wash, and a dining room full of hungry, impatient, traveling men to feed."

A train whistled in the distance.

"That'll be Number Five, Emma," Mr. Cooley called from the seat of the wagon. "We'd best make tracks, or we'll have some unhappy customers."

"Good-bye, Laura," Mrs. Cooley called out. "Come and see us soon. Anytime at all. We can go to church some Sunday, and see about that choir."

"We will, Emma," Mama said. Both families waved good-bye. "Thank you all so much," Mama said. "We will never forget this day."

Mama's face glowed as they watched the Cooleys drive away.

Finally, Mama, Papa, and Rose were alone again. The woods seemed very still after all that commotion.

"Let's take a look, shall we?" said Papa. They walked all the way around the barn. It was the first time Rose had seen all its sides. It was much bigger than she had expected. Where Papa and Cyrus had laid logs to make two squares in the grass, there were now two log rooms. In between the rooms was an open hallway. That was where Papa would put the wagon and store the harness to keep it dry. Over all of it was the shingled roof. Seeing the roof made Rose feel happy; from now on the horses would be safe and dry. But the barn was not chinked. Rose could see in through the wide spaces between the logs.

"Won't the horses get cold?" Rose asked. "Don't we have to put mud in the cracks, like the house?"

"No," Papa said. "This is the way they build barns here. It's not so cold and windy as South Dakota."

Rose ran into the open hallway and saw four large openings, two on either side. She looked into one of them. The large room was divided in half by a log wall. She looked in all the doorways and saw that both rooms were the same. The barn had been divided into four stalls, one for each of the horses.

The stall openings needed gates, but Papa said he would do that later. The air there was rich with the sweet scent of new-cut wood. Rose took a deep breath to enjoy it better.

Mama walked into all the stalls, touching the wood and looking at the workmanship.

"They did a solid job," said Mama. "It should last us a long, long time."

"Yes, and the wood is green," said Papa. "When the logs dry out and shrink, the joints will be even tighter."

"Oh, Manly," Mama said, turning to look at Papa with shining eyes. "Who could ask for better neighbors?"

Rose had not thought about it all day, in the excitement and confusion. But now she asked, "Why did all those strangers come to help build our barn?"

"It's a custom in these hills," Papa said. "They call it a working, Rose, when folks get together to help each other with some big chore. It's a chance to be sociable with your neighbors and do them a good turn at the same time. These Ozarkers know that everyone needs a hand sometime. It just happened to be our turn."

Rose remembered Mama reading from Romans: "Be of the same mind one toward another."

"But how could we ever help all those people back?" she asked. "There were so many."

"We'll be living here a long time, Rose,"

Mama said. "There will be no end of chances to show our thanks."

The forest darkened as the sun set. A few crimson-and-gold clouds floated in the clear sky. Rose helped Papa spread straw and dry leaves on the earthen floor of the new stalls. Then he led the horses in for the first time. Pet walked right in, her head held high. Little Pet tried to follow, but Papa pushed her out.

"You youngsters are getting too old to stable with your mothers," Papa said. "It's time you were weaned and on your own." While Mama tied Pet to a log in her stall, Papa tied a rope on Little Pet and led her into her own stall next door. Little Pet whinnied and defiantly tossed her head as Papa tied her to a log, too. But when the colt saw her mother in the stall opposite, she calmed down.

After Papa and Mama had put May and Prince into their stalls, Papa visited each of the four horses. He talked softly to them and stroked their necks, to make them feel at home. When Mama, Papa, and Rose finally left the barn, the horses watched them go, peering at them through the openings in the logs.

"We're as poor as mice in the spring," Mama said over supper. "Yet now I know we aren't alone here. I suppose we aren't having such a hard time after all." Her beautiful purple-blue eyes sparkled in the lamplight. "It depends on how you look at it."

"Yes, indeed!" said Papa. "It depends a good deal on how you look at it."

Rose thought about the lonely log house that had first greeted them. They had no cows or sheep yet. But Rocky Ridge was a real farm now, with a dry, sturdy place for the mares and colts, a comfortable henhouse for the chickens, and a tightly chinked house for themselves.

Coming to Missouri had been a wonderful adventure after all. Rose wished Grandma, Grandpa, and her aunts could see Rocky Ridge Farm. She knew they would be just as proud of it as she was.

Author's Note

Dear Reader,

Since 1968, thousands of children have written to me. That's when Rose Wilder Lane died at the age of eighty-one, leaving me, her only heir, all the "Little House" books written by her mother, Laura Ingalls Wilder. Many of those letters express the same feelings—that Laura seems like a friend, and that her books make readers feel as though they are a part of her life.

I have tried in this book, and the others that will soon follow, to do the same for Rose's life. I loved Rose just like a grandmother. In fact, I called her Gramma. I sat in her warm, cozy kitchen many times watching her knead dough to bake bread, or browning chicken for her famous chicken pie, and talking with her about things that were bothering me, about writing, about the world, the weather, and life.

Like Laura, Rose was a great writer. She knew that to write well about something, you had to be sure of your facts, even when writing about yourself. It is easier to make a book seem real when it is about your own life, as Laura's are. But this book is not about my life, or even about my lifetime.

To make *Little House on Rocky Ridge* seem as real as Laura's books, I had to learn things about Rose's life when she was a little girl, long before I was born. There were some stories that she had told me herself. But I also read her diaries and letters and the many stories and books she wrote when she was grown up. And I had to learn about life in 1894, the year this story takes place. I had to make sure of my facts.

So that is how it came to be that many people actually helped me to write this book. Some of them were experts about history. They told me what living was really like one hundred years ago, when Laura and Almanzo brought Rose to Missouri. Some of them knew about farm life and told me all about chickens and horses and such. Some people who helped me were good friends, who kept my spirits up. There were other writers, too, who showed me what was good about my writing, and how to make it better.

There isn't room here to thank all those people. But here are a few who were especially helpful:

William Anderson, a schoolteacher and writer who has worked for years to preserve and protect the memory of Laura and Rose;

Bonnie Appleby, my assistant and trusted friend;

Eddie Bell, Chief Executive Officer of HarperCollins UK, who encouraged me to write this book and was determined to publish it;

Norma Lee Browning Ogg, a protégé and good friend of Rose's;

Jean Coday, head of the elementary school in Rose's old hometown and one of my dearest friends;

Robert B. Flanders, Ph.D., and Robert K.

Gilmore, Ph.D., experts on the history of the Ozark Mountains of Missouri, at the Center for Ozark Studies in Springfield;

Erin Gathrid, my editor at HarperCollins, who always held me to the highest standards set by Laura's books;

Vivian Glover, curator of the Laura Ingalls Wilder Memorial Society in De Smet, South Dakota, a long-time inspiration to all who know her;

Dwight M. Miller, the person in charge of keeping most of Laura's and Rose's diaries and writings at the Herbert Hoover Presidential Library in West Branch, Iowa;

Neta Seal, an old friend of Laura's who told me tales of her own childhood growing up in the early years of this century in the Ozarks;

Noel Silverman, my close friend and valued attorney;

And Connie Tidwell, late curator of the museum and homestead at Mansfield, Missouri, where Laura and Almanzo settled in 1894.

Homecoming by Cynthia Voigt
£3.50

Dicey made her announcement to James, Sammy and Maybeth: "We're going to have to walk all the way to Bridgeport." But they had no money and the whole world was arranged for people who had money – or rather, for adults who had money. The world was arranged against kids. Well, she could handle it. She'd have to. Somehow.

Dicey's Song by Cynthia Voigt
£3.50

Still troubled about her mother, and anxious about the three younger children, Dicey seems to have no time for growing up – until an incident at school shows her what to do.

A Solitary Blue by Cynthia Voigt
£3.50

Jeff has always been a loner, ever since his mother walked out, leaving him with his taciturn and distant father. Then his mother invites him to Charleston. For one glorious summer, Jeff is happy, before his dreams are shattered.

The Runner by Cynthia Voigt
£3.50

Bullet Tillerman has little interest in anyone or anything except running. But this is the 1960s, and with racial war at home and the Vietnam War abroad, Bullet's beliefs have to change, particularly when he's asked to coach a new black runner at the school.

Harriet the Spy by Louise Fitzhugh
£3.50

"I'm a spy that writes down everything," says eleven-year-old Harriet, as she fills her secret notebook with ruthlessly honest observations about her friends and the people around her. The trouble starts when her friends find her notebook...

The Fib by George Layton
£2.99

"I was sick of Gordon Barraclough going on about my old football gear. So I told him it had belonged to my uncle, Bobby Charlton! That was the fib. Then a few days later, we met Bobby Charlton..." Eight short, funny stories about many important issues of adolescent life – school, girlfriends, football, and the problems of keeping in with your mates and getting round Mum.

My Mate Shofiq by Jan Needle
£2.99

When Bernard witnesses the quiet Pakistani boy, Shofiq, defending some younger curry kids against a bully and his gang, he is gradually drawn into friendship with him and discovers they share the same problems at home too. The violent clash between Bernard's gang and the bullies, and the break-up of Shofiq's family under pressure from the authorities, lead to a dramatic and thought-provoking climax.

Harriet the Spy
by Louise Fitzhugh

Harriet the Spy has a secret notebook, which she fills with utterly honest jottings about her parents, her friends and her neighbours. Every day on her spy route, she scrutinises, observes and notes down anything of interest :

Laura Peters is thinner and uglier. I think she could do with some braces on her teeth.

If Marion Hawthorne doesn't watch out she's going to grow up into a lady Hitler.

But Harriet commits the unforgivable for a spy – she is unmasked. When her notebook is found by her school friends, their anger and retaliation and Harriet's unexpected responses explode in a hilarious and often touching way.

£3.50

Order Form

To order direct from the publishers, just make a list of the titles you want and fill in the form below:

Name ....

Address ....

....

....

Send to: Dept 6, HarperCollins Publishers Ltd, Westerhill Road, Bishopbriggs, Glasgow G64 2QT.

Please enclose a cheque or postal order to the value of the cover price, plus:

UK & BFPO: Add £1.00 for the first book, and 25p per copy for each addition book ordered.

Overseas and Eire: Add £2.95 service charge. Books will be sent by surface mail but quotes for airmail despatch will be given on request.

A 24-hour telephone ordering service is avail-able to Visa and Access card holders: 041-772 2281